"You Used Me, Kailin!

"You loved the excitement I brought into your life, you loved the danger and you loved playing at rebellion. But you didn't love me. I wasn't good enough for you, remember? Quentin J. Yarbro's high-society daughter could take a roll in the hay with a country vet's son, but she sure as hell wasn't going to marry him."

Kailin looked up to find Brett staring down at her. His gaze caressed her face like the touch of a hand. "We could have had it all, Kailin," he continued softly. "I loved you so much it hurts just to think about it. But you threw it away."

"You never told me," she insisted. "You never once said the words, Brett. Never once."

Something like pain flickered across his features. "I guess you're right. Somehow, I thought that if you loved someone enough, you didn't have to say anything."

"Are you happy now?" Kailin simply had to ask.

He smiled a grim little smile that scarcely moved his lips. "Does it matter?"

Dear Reader:

Welcome! You hold in your hand a Silhouette Desire—your ticket to a whole new world of reading pleasure.

A Silhouette Desire is a sensuous, contemporary romance about passions, problems and the ultimate power of love. It is about today's woman—intelligent, successful, giving—but it is also the story of a romance between two people who are strong enough to follow their own individual paths, yet strong enough to compromise, as well.

These books are written by, for and about every woman that you are—wife, mother, sister, lover, daughter, career woman. A Silhouette Desire heroine must face the same challenges, achieve the same successes, in her story as you do in your own life.

The Silhouette reader is not afraid to enjoy herself. She knows when to take things seriously and when to indulge in a fantasy world. With six books a month, Silhouette Desire strives to meet her many moods, but each book is always a compelling love story.

Make a commitment to romance—go wild with Silhouette Desire!

Best,

Isabel Swift
Senior Editor & Editorial Coordinator

NAOMI HORTON
Crossfire

Silhouette Desire

Published by Silhouette Books New York

America's Publisher of Contemporary Romance

SILHOUETTE BOOKS
300 East 42nd St., New York, N.Y. 10017

ISBN: 0-373-05435-1

First Silhouette Books printing July 1988

Printed in the U.S.A.

NAOMI HORTON

was born in northern Alberta, where the winters are long and the libraries far apart. "When I'd run out of books," she says, "I'd simply create my own—entire worlds filled with people, adventure and romance. I guess it's not surprising that I'm still at it!" An engineering technologist, she currently lives in Toronto with her collection of assorted pets.

Prologue

I'm pregnant."

How she got the words out, Kailin didn't know. She listened to the fading echo of her voice as though it belonged to someone else and watched the tall, bearded young man standing by the window stiffen. Slowly he turned his head to stare at her.

"Pregnant?" His voice was soft with disbelief. "How?"

Kailin had to smile in spite of being nearer tears than laughter. "You're the veterinary student, Brett. And you'll have to agree that we haven't always been as careful as we...we should have been."

The heavy beard did nothing to hide the flush that touched his handsome features. But even as numbed as she was, it took Kailin only a moment to realize that it was anger burning his cheeks, not embarrassment. She stared at him in bewilderment, her initial awkwardness giving way to unease as he made no move toward her. She'd expected him to be surprised, perhaps even momentarily angry at their mutual carelessness, but not once in the past two night-mare weeks had she anticipated such cold remoteness.

The blue eyes that had been filled with love in the past were hard now, and a little cold. "You're lying, Kailin."

It was her turn to stare in disbelief. "What?" Her voice was thin and high.

Brett's smile was humorless. "You're good, Kailin. You're real good." He sauntered across to his ancient brown sofa and dropped onto it, stretching his jean-clad legs out in front of him and draping both arms along the back of the sofa as he gazed coolly across the room at her. "Your old man was here a couple of hours ago."

Kailin blinked, feeling curiously light-headed. "Daddy was here?"

The corner of Brett's mouth tipped up even further, his eyes cutting. "He told me you're not pregnant at all, Kailin." The faint smile might have held a trace of honest humor for a moment. "Your old man doesn't like me much, Kailin. Apparently a troublemaker from the wrong side of the tracks isn't quite what he had in mind for his only daughter."

"Brett!"

"You've been using me." The smile vanished, and in its place was a hardness she'd never seen on that lean, hand-some face before. "You've been flaunting me in front of your rich friends like a dog on a leash. And I've been great ammunition in that firefight you've been waging with your father all summer. He told me all about it—how every time you two have an argument you threaten to run off with me. How you've been keeping him 'in line,' as he put it. He also told me that he's tired of it and has called your bluff. He warned me, man-to-man, that I was being used, and not to fall for it too seriously."

Stunned, Kailin shook her head numbly. "Brett," she finally managed to whisper, "that's not what I—"

Brett lunged to his feet. "What game are we playing now, Kailin?" he demanded. "Am I supposed to toss you out into the street so you can run home to Daddy and get his sympathy? Or am I supposed to marry you? God, that would really drive your father nuts, wouldn't it?" He paced to the window, his body taut with anger. "It would be the ultimate act of rebellion, all right. Next to *actually* getting pregnant, that is." He looked around at her, his mouth wrenched in that bitter smile again. "And I wouldn't even put that past you, Kailin. You're as twisted and manipulative as he is. But don't expect me to play this one out to the end, baby, because I'm tired of your games."

"Brett—" The name was no more than a harsh sob torn from her. "You can't believe—!"

"Oh, I believe," he said softly, his eyes shadowed with pain. "There's just one thing I'd like to know, Kailin. Was any of it real? When we were making love and you'd say all those things—did you ever, even just once, mean any of it? Or was it all just part of the game?"

One

This isn't some silly game you're playing! So will you shape up and stop acting like such an idiot?''

Kailin glared at her own reflection in the mirror above the dressing table. God! Half a pound of blusher and twice her usual amount of eye shadow and lipstick and she still looked like a terrified eighteen-year-old on the first day of a new job. Where in hell was the cool, self-possessed business-woman who was under there *somewhere*?

Cool? Self-possessed? Kailin managed a grim smile. She'd been about as far from self-possessed as it was possible to get ever since she'd stepped off that plane in Fort Myers three days ago. And any remnants of bravery that had survived that far had dissipated completely during the five-mile drive across the causeway to Sanibel Island. She was, in a word, a wreck.

"You should have told them no," she muttered for the umpteenth time that morning. It was the same refrain she'd been repeating for nearly seven weeks, ever since she'd found out the unpleasant little truth behind why her father had *really* recommended her for this job.

"He set me up," she found herself whispering. She glared at the wide-eyed woman in the mirror and took a deep breath. "And you, you idiot! You walked right into it. Why didn't you just stand up to the whole lot of them and tell them no?"

Except that she had. She'd told the Miami bank executives two or three times that she didn't care if the Paradise Point investors *and* their trouble-fraught resort complex was sucked into the vortex of the Bermuda Triangle, she was *not* getting involved. She was an industrial management troubleshooter, not a miracle worker. Her job was to go in and save companies that were sliding toward disaster because of bad management or outdated production methods or faulty quality control—*not* to bail banks out of bad investment choices.

What the bankers hadn't known, of course, was that it wasn't them she was refusing to help, but her father. Quentin Yarbro had gotten himself into serious trouble this time. Trouble that he wasn't going to be able to bluff or bully his way out of, and she'd been looking forward to seeing him brought down by his own greed. A fitting end, all things considered.

Kailin gave a snort of laughter and started brushing her thick, shoulder-length hair furiously. In the end she'd caved in, exactly as he'd known she would. With the fortitude of wet cardboard, she'd capitulated even while swearing she wouldn't and had stalked out of that bank boardroom in a simmering rage at her own spinelessness, contract in hand.

The bankers and their desperate clients, that small group of people—her father among them—who had invested cold, hard cash in the Paradise Point development, were delighted and relieved. Paradise Point was in serious trouble, and with it a hair-raising amount of investors' money. They needed someone to go down to Sanibel Island who was used to salvaging businesses on the verge of bankruptcy. Someone who could go in and pinpoint the trouble spots and plug the holes before the entire ship sank and left everyone—developer and investor alike—floundering around in unfriendly waters.

Someone like Kailin McGuire.

It was her father who had recommended her to the bank and investors; her father who had explained everything to her and had finally pleaded with her to help.

Except he hadn't told her one thing.

He hadn't told her about Brett Douglass.

Kailin's stomach tightened. She closed her eyes and forced herself to relax. So far this morning she'd managed not to think of him. Well, not more than six or seven dozen times, anyway. But every time she *did* think of him, her stomach gave that same sick little twist. As she had a hundred times during the past three days, she looked yearningly at the empty suitcases standing by the door. She could be packed and halfway across the causeway to Fort Myers in an hour; on a plane back to Indiana in another two. The Paradise Point developers could find someone else to bail them out, the Miami bank and the rest of the investors could find someone else to salvage their money, and Brett...Brett Douglass wouldn't even have to know she'd been here.

Kailin, Kailin...don't go. Don't...

It was his own voice, echoing off the walls of his bedroom like a cry from the past. It faded into the darkness, leaving him wide-awake and sweating and cursing softly.

He sat up and stared bleakly into the dark of the room, still breathing fast, his heart racing like a runaway flywheel.

Kailin. Always, the dreams were of Kailin. Bad, wild dreams that left him shaking and sweating in the night, so filled with anger and loss that his very soul ached with it.

This one had been no different from all the others. They'd fought, the bitter, angry words the same as always. Kailin's tears glittering just as they had that night. At the end, when she'd turned away and her eyes had caught his for an instant, huge and filled with hurt and betrayal, he'd felt something splinter inside him. That, too, was the way it had happened.

But then the dreams always veered off from reality into a special nightmare of their own. Unlike what had really happened on that night eleven years ago, he went after her in the dreams. He would sprint across the room and snatch the door before it slammed shut, then run out into the street and try to call out to her, to follow. But he would be trapped in that special slow-motion dreamtime, like a fly in amber, unable to move or shout, watching as Kailin disappeared. The woman he'd loved as much as life itself.

And had hated as deeply.

Brett drew in a deep, careful breath, the ache like a hard, bitter stone under his heart. Eleven years. One would almost think that a man should be able to shake free of a woman after eleven years. "Damn you, Kailin," he whispered into the empty darkness, the ache higher now, in the back of his throat. "Damn you, why won't you leave me alone?"

She should have left well enough alone.

Kailin thought suddenly of her father. Right now he was probably sitting in his study up in Greenlake, Indiana, chuckling about how clever he'd been. He had known that Brett was down here. That's *really* why he'd recommended her for this job: not because he believed she was the best person to handle it, or even because of some faint paternal pride, but simply because he thought it would give Paradise Point an advantage, an edge....

Advantages. Edges. Those were the only terms her father understood. Things like fair play and trust and honor were as alien to him as his way of doing business was to her. Yet somehow they were on the same side this time.

In spite of herself, Kailin smiled. It seemed strange, fighting *for* her father instead of simply fighting him. They'd been at each other's throats for so many years that she couldn't remember a time when they'd been anything but bitter opponents. Even as a child, she'd fought and fought: the rules, the reasons, the way things were. She'd called him rigid and authoritarian; he'd called her irresponsible and disobedient. She'd called it growing up, he'd called it rebelliousness, and they'd even fought over the naming of it.

It had gotten worse that last summer. That was the summer she'd fallen in love with Brett Douglass, and the battles between her and her father had escalated into all-out warfare.

Kailin's smile widened. She and Brett had been a study in classic chemistry, the pull between them so strong it had raised sparks. They'd made an eye-catching couple, all right, she blond and rich and very much from the right side of town, he dark and bearded, a born rebel out to change the world. They'd come together like colliding comets, and those sparks had turned incendiary, exploding into a passion that had left them both shaken.

And burned, Kailin reminded herself.

The smile slipped. She drew in a deep breath and was annoyed to feel her eyes sting. She blinked the sudden tears away angrily and pulled the brush through her hair again with long, savage strokes. "Why don't you grow up!" she hissed at her reflection. "So you fell in love and got hurt. So what? It happens all the time. You're not that stupid nineteen-year-old anymore—it's been eleven years. He probably doesn't even remember you!"

The brush hit a knot and she wrenched it free roughly, her eyes filling with tears again at the sharp pain. "It's too late now, anyway," she muttered as she rubbed her scalp with her fingers. "You took on this project and you're stuck with it. So start worrying about how you're going to keep this Paradise Point thing from falling apart, and *stop* worrying about a man you haven't seen in over a decade."

To her relief, the pep talk worked. For a moment or two at least, the nerves-of-steel businesswoman took over. The green eyes that met hers in the mirror were calm now and filled with a steady determination that flirted with outright stubbornness. There was a jut to the square jaw that boded ill for anyone rash enough to underestimate either the mind or the iron will behind it. Becky called it her Wonder Woman Look.

Again Kailin had to laugh. She turned away from the mirror with a toss of her head and strode across the room, snatching up her handbag and briefcase from the bed on her way by. Did Wonder Woman ever get a run in her last pair of panty hose or forget to pay her parking tickets or get lost on a Los Angeles freeway and wind up in Santa Barbara when she was supposed to be going to San Diego? And would Wonder Woman ever sit through four consecutive showings of *Top Gun* because her nine-year-old daughter had a world-class crush on Tom Cruise, or cancel a business meeting at the last minute to go kite flying with that same daughter, or still delight in building sand castles?

Probably not. But then, who wanted to be Wonder Woman, anyway?

Brett parked his pickup truck in the shade beside the old church that now housed his veterinary practice and turned off the engine, noticing that his hand was trembling slightly. Damn it, what was happening to him? He made no move to get out of the truck, still solidly shaken by what he'd seen. Or by what he *thought* he'd seen.

Kailin...

Brett took a deep breath. No. He'd seen *someone*, all right, but it hadn't been Kailin.

All he'd seen was a tantalizing glimpse of wind-tangled hair and honey-gold flesh. God knew, there was hardly a shortage of either on Sanibel this time of year.

He wrenched open the truck door and got out, his footsteps crunching on the crushed coral and shell that made up the driveway. Talcum-powder dust rose in small puffs behind him, hanging languorously in the still, hot air. Besides, he reminded himself as he took the front steps two at a time, she'd probably cut that gorgeous mane of sunbleached hair by now. She'd worn it loose back then, in a thick torrent that the Indiana sun had turned a hundred shades of silver and gold. He could remember how she would run her fingers through it and scoop it off her face with a toss of her head, then give that quick, flirtatious glance that had half the men in town falling all over themselves.

Damn it, will you stop brooding about her? He wrenched the door to the clinic open and a blast of air hit him, arctic after the tropical heat outside. What the hell was the matter with him, anyway? Kailin Yarbro—Kailin *McGuire* now, he reminded himself bitterly—had walked out of his life eleven years ago. He was eleven years older and wiser now, and surely past the point where an unexpected glimpse of long tanned legs and a cascade of sun-silvered hair could still turn him inside out. Just how long, he found himself speculating ferociously, did it take for a bruised heart to heal?

There was the scamper of small feet and an explosion of delighted barking as Artoo, the tiny mostly-terrier mongrel that had adopted the clinic, came tearing around the corner. He lost traction on the polished floor and went spinning out of control, then scrambled to his feet and tore headlong at Brett's ankles, tongue and ears flying.

Brett laughed and scooped him up in one hand. "Take it easy, youngster."

"How are you with bees?" The cheerful voice of his assistant fluted from the door of the tiny office cum waiting room.

"Bees?" He walked into the office and looked at Kathy Fischer warily, depositing the excited Artoo on her desk. "What kind of bees?"

"Wild bees." She tossed him a clean white lab coat, not even missing a beat as she deftly rescued a telephone bill that was disappearing into Artoo's mouth. "Workers putting in the foundation for that new condo at the end of Island Inn Road unearthed a hive this morning. They've swarmed—the bees, I mean—and the construction crew refuses to go back to work until someone gets rid of them."

"Me," Brett groaned. "Why do they always call me?"

"Because everyone knows you're the best veterinarian in Florida," Kathy said teasingly. "Maybe on the entire East Coast. And everyone knows that veterinarians have a special way with creatures." She laughed at Brett's eloquent look. "The foreman's been calling here every twenty minutes. He says he's losing eight hundred dollars an hour and that you can name your price if you'll move the swarm so his men can go back to work."

"I wouldn't touch them if he named the place after me," Brett muttered as he pulled on the lab coat. "Give old Jonas Merriweather a call. He used to raise bees. I've seen him move a swarm with his bare hands.... The man's nuttier than a fruitcake."

At that moment Artoo stuck his face enthusiastically into a mug on the corner of Kathy's desk. Recoiling with a sneeze that sprayed cold coffee in all directions, he promptly backed off the desk. He landed on the floor with a surprised yelp, paper cascading around him, then snatched one end of a streamer of adding machine tape and raced out the door with it.

"That," Kathy said calmly, nodding toward the door, "was this month's accounts receivable." She smiled as she picked up the scattered mail from the floor. "You've got a visitor."

Brett felt the hair on the back of his neck stir.

He walked to the window, pretending to look out at something with eyes squeezed shut. What was happening to him? First the dream, then—

"Who?" he asked abruptly, not looking around.

If Kathy heard anything unusual in his voice, she didn't let on. "Zac Cheevers. Something about Paradise Point."

Brett hadn't known he was holding his breath until he released it in a *huff* of relief. How long, he wondered, would the impact of last night's dream stay with him? Sometimes it lasted for days.

"I sent him down to your office."

"Thanks, Kath." Brett glanced around to smile at her, finding her gazing at him with a faint frown.

"Is, uh...everything all right? You look a little...pale."

Silently cursing the intuitive abilities of women in general, and Kathy's in particular, Brett held his smile firmly in place. "Nothing about twelve hours of sleep wouldn't cure," he lied, heading for the door. "I got together with a couple of old friends last night, and we watched the sun come up over a bottle of good Scotch and a lot of reminiscing."

"Oh." Kathy's face cleared, and she laughed. "Hunt and Jill Kincaide, I'll bet. Jill called yesterday to tell me they were on Sanibel again for a few days. What's the baby like?"

"Small and noisy." He grinned at Kathy's look of outrage and stepped into the corridor before she could quiz him further. Jill and Hunter *had* come over the previous night, but they'd left well before midnight.

I don't know what the hell's wrong with you, Douglass, he muttered to himself as he walked down the corridor. It's been eleven years, for crying out loud. Last night was just a dream, and this morning was just ... what?

A mirage, he told himself brutally. Wishful thinking. It didn't matter. Whoever that woman had been, she hadn't been Kailin McGuire.

Without even wanting to, he found himself thinking of the way she'd looked that first time he'd seen her: tall and cat-lithe, skin burnished by a summer's worth of sailing and tennis, that magnificent mane of silver-gold hair tousled and loose. She'd been one of a bunch of college kids piled into a baby-blue Mercedes convertible, all of them laughing and windblown as they'd cruised slowly by the besieged gates of Yarbro Paint and Chemicals. They'd radiated the lazy arrogance that comes with the right address, the right car, the right college, and it hadn't taken him more than one look to know that she was rich and spoiled and more trouble than any one man needed.

But one look was all it had taken. He hadn't known then that she was the daughter of the very man whose chemical plant he and his environmentalist friends were picketing. He doubted it would have made any difference. The protest had been one of many they'd staged that summer. By then they, Yarbro's security people and the police had had the entire thing down to a well-choreographed ballet: gates picketed, speeches given, fists shaken, everyone lazy and good-natured in the heat of high summer. Every protest had brought out a parade of passersby—some to support, some to jeer, others simply to stare curiously. Then, that late afternoon, along had come the woman who would change his life.

Warned of trouble, Yarbro's men had closed the high chain-link gates barring the only road into the plant, which was exactly what Brett had been counting on. He'd chained himself securely to those same gates, and what had been designed as a barricade to keep troublemakers like him *out* had worked just as effectively to keep the two big tanker trucks filled with chemical waste *in*. It had been a grand-standing gesture, done more for media attention than in any real hope of stopping Yarbro from polluting the river.

But this time it had caught more than just media attention. The blue convertible had slowed as it had passed the gates, and he'd held his breath as eyes the color of new grass had met his, appraising and faintly amused. She'd taken in the tattered Marine camouflage jacket, the beard, the heavy chain around his waist. Then those dark-lashed eyes had settled on his again, filled with challenge and teasing promise and laughter. Unable to stop himself, he'd swept off an imaginary hat and had flourished it in a sweeping, extravagant bow, and when he'd straightened, grinning broadly, he'd been rewarded with a small, private smile that had told him he'd be seeing her again, and that he could count on it.

She'd been true to that unspoken promise. And he'd been right: Kailin Yarbro had been more trouble than any one man needed.

Brett suddenly realized that he was standing at the door to his office—and had been for the past few minutes, unmoving, hand on the knob. Mentally he'd been a thousand miles to the north, standing under the blazing Indiana sun, falling madly in love.

Love. Brett gave a derisive snort and opened his office door, shaking off his pensive mood as a dog shakes off water. Whatever he and Kailin had shared during that long, steamy summer in Greenlake, it hadn't been love.

"About time you showed up." The man seated beside Brett's desk tossed aside the magazine he'd been looking through. "I was beginning to wonder if you were coming in at all."

"It's good to see you, too, Zac," Brett told him dryly. "Get you a cup of coffee?"

"Got one," Zac rasped, shifting his dead cigar to the other corner of his mouth. "Your life-style's going to kill you, boy. You look like hell. Hope she was worth losin' a night's sleep for.''

''My life-style's just fine,'' Brett replied with a pointed look at Zac's cigar. ''And it wasn't a woman that kept me up half the night.'' *Not a real one, anyway,* he added silently. ''If I did even half the carousing I get accused of doing around here, I'd have died of exhaustion long ago.''

The rolls of extra flesh around Zac's ample middle rocked with laughter. Then his expression sobered and he shoved a manila file folder across the desk. ''Well, here's something that'll keep you up nights. They've thrown us a curve, Douglass.''

''Who?'' Brett eased himself into his swivel desk chair and reached across to pick up the folder.

''Paradise Point, what else?'' Zac's voice was bitter. ''The Land Use Committee got a call last night from that bank in Miami representing the investors backing the resort. They've brought in a mediator as a last-ditch effort to keep the project afloat—an industrial management consultant or some damn thing. Anyway, seems they're going to try to work up some sort of compromise between us—the Land Use Committee, I mean—and Gulf Coast.''

''Compromise?'' Frowning, Brett flipped the folder open and started perusing the contents. ''What kind of compromise?''

''We won't know that until this afternoon. This mediator or whatever called to set up a meeting with us at three.''

''And Gulf Coast? Are they going to be there?''

''From what I heard, Gulf Coast isn't very happy about it, but they'll be there. The bank told them to cooperate—or else.''

Brett smiled, a trifle grimly. ''So the investors are playing hardball, are they?''

''There's a lot of money tied up in Paradise Point. If Gulf Coast folds, that money's gone out with the tide. Guess they're hoping to salvage something." Zac gave a snort. "Damned fools."

"Maybe not," Brett said quietly. "Nobody wants to see Paradise Point fold. Phase One of the development is one of the most successful on Sanibel."

"Old age turnin' you soft, boy?" Zac asked in astonishment. "When you first showed up on Sanibel you were a real fire-eater. I remember watchin' you go a full ten rounds with any developer not toeing the line. Without you we wouldn't even *have* a Land Use Committee." The cigar shifted. "Hell, boy, you were the one hollering the loudest about gettin' Gulf Coast shut down."

"I want Craig Bryant shut down, not the company. Gulf Coast has always done right by us, you know that."

"Craig's daddy's always done right by us, you mean," Zac growled. "That pup of his ain't worth toad spit." He skewered Brett with an assessing look. "You know as well as I do that Phase Two of the Paradise Point project is garbage. Are you sayin' we should go ahead and approve Phase Three anyway?"

"I'm just saying we shouldn't toss the gold out with the dross. If there's a chance we can get Gulf Coast to clean up its act, it would be as much in our favor as theirs to get Paradise Point finished. And that's impossible unless we approve Phase Three." Brett smiled. "It doesn't cost us anything to listen to what they have to say, Zac."

Zac gave a grunt, but then he nodded and stood up. He took the folder when Brett held it out. "Three o'clock sharp. Douglass. Big meeting room in back of my place."

"What does this mediator sound like, anyway?" Brett asked as Zac walked to the door. "Like he knows what he's doing?"

"Sounds like any other three-piece-suiter," Zac muttered darkly. "Talking about profit-loss margins and bottom lines and a bunch of other stuff I only half understood.

And it ain't a he, it's a she. Sounds keen, too. Too damned keen for my taste.''

"She?'' Brett looked up with interest. "Miss or Mrs.?''

Zac's beefy face broke into a broad grin. "That sounds more like the Brett Douglass I know,'' he said with a chuckle. "Though from the little bit I spent talkin' with her, I'd say you'd be wastin' your time. Ice-cold, and brittle as steel—it's *Ms.*—Ms. McGuire.''

"McGuire?'' Brett felt himself turn cold, his mouth suddenly dry. Impossible, he told himself numbly.

"Yeah.'' Zac paused in the doorway. "Kay something, think she said. Could've been Kaitlin.''

"Kailin,'' Brett corrected automatically, hardly aware he'd said anything at all.

Nearly three o'clock.

Kailin dragged her eyes from the big wall clock above the far end of the meeting table, so on edge that she felt like screaming. Premeeting jitters, she told herself firmly. That was all it was. Once everyone was here and they got started, she would be fine.

Unable to stand still, she wandered across to the long, low windows running the full length of the elegantly appointed meeting room. They overlooked a landscaped garden filled with palmettos, giant scarlet hibiscus and a hundred other flowering shrubs and vines. Along one side, two flamboyant Hong Kong orchid trees dripped loose petals across the grass. It was eerily still as though the whole world were holding its breath. Kailin looked at the sky with apprehension.

Sullen cobalt clouds seemed to press earthward, and Kailin thought uneasily of the tropical storm that had come bellowing up through the Keys and into the Gulf the week before. It hadn't quite reached full hurricane status before it had blown itself out, but it had done enough damage to convince her that she didn't want to be down here when another one hit.

Storm warnings. Kailin smiled. They'd been going off in her mind all day, presaging a hurricane of a different sort. Her own reflection stared back at her against the steel-blue sky, and she realized with a jolt that she looked scared to death.

She sighed and reached up to brush her hair back from her forehead, taking a deep breath and trying to compose herself. It was too late to go back now. They would all be here in a few minutes, and she had a job to do. The only thing that should be concerning her right now was Paradise Point.

A mutter of thunder made her glance at the sky again. For some reason the threatening clouds made her think of the last time she'd seen Brett. That night eleven years ago, when it had all come to an end, as everything finally does.

Kailin shook her head, sending the memories scattering. Enough of that. It had all happened a long time ago, to a woman she couldn't even remember being. A lot had happened since: marriage; a baby lost and a baby born; the car accident that had left her widowed; the struggle that had followed. She'd grown up fast. She'd put the past to rest as best she could, had fought herself free—or almost free—of her father's bullying domination, had made a comfortable home for herself and Becky and had become one of the top management troubleshooters in the country. She was on Sanibel Island on business, and there was no way that anything—not past mistakes, not guilt, not even revenge—was going to mess that up.

Something moved behind her. Another reflection joined hers on the storm-darkened glass, and Kailin suddenly went cold.

Even though she'd expected it, she wasn't prepared for the reality of seeing him again. He was standing so close to her that she could feel his heat radiate through the thin silk of her blouse, could feel the intimate warmth of his breath on the back of her neck. He used to kiss her there. Slow, tickling kisses that had made her melt while he'd stroked and caressed her breasts, her stomach, then lower still....

She closed her eyes, grasping the windowsill when her knees threatened to give out. Hesitantly, half expecting the image to have vanished, she looked up.

He smiled. It was a slow, almost mocking smile. "Hello, Kailin."

His voice was the same. Deep and quiet, with that rough-timbred purr to it that had driven every woman she'd ever known wild. He had a voice, a friend of hers had once said, that made love to you while he was just saying hello.

"Brett." The name was still magic in her mouth. Only this time, finally, he was there to answer it, not simply a memory in the night.

He must have heard some of that in the one word, because for an instant the years between them vanished. His gaze burned into hers, as raw and vital and hungry as it had ever been, and he seemed to sway toward her. She held her breath, waiting for his touch.

Two

It never came. As suddenly as the electric awareness had sparked between them it was gone. Something shuttered across his eyes, and although he hadn't moved a muscle, it was as though he were suddenly across the room from her. He stepped away, and Kailin closed her eyes again, took a deep breath and turned around.

Brett was leaning against the far wall, hands shoved in the pockets of his jeans, one long leg bent slightly at the knee. He looked the picture of relaxation, gazing calmly at her across the barricade of the long oak table.

It was disconcerting how little he'd changed. The beard was gone, but she'd expected that. She found herself staring at him, fascinated, and realized suddenly that it was the first time she'd ever seen his bare face. It was straight-featured and lean, with the high, strong Iroquois cheekbones he'd inherited from his great-grandmother. His hair was much shorter than it had been. Tidily and expensively trimmed, it curled around his ears and the back of his neck and, as always, lay across his forehead in beguiling disarray, as though just disturbed by a woman's loving touch. His eyes were the same, that vivid blue that—like a prairie sky—seemed to darken with his mood, warmly azure one moment and storm-indigo the next. They were an odd in-between right now, and curiously flat.

That cool, steady stare unnerved her. She feigned a smile and walked to the head of the table, taking the papers from her slim leather portfolio as though she had absolutely nothing on her mind but this meeting. "I wondered if you'd come."

There was a quiet chuckle, more malevolent than amused. "You couldn't have kept me away, Kailin."

She gave him a quick, nervous glance. He had shrugged away from the wall and was prowling the room, pausing by the windows to stare out into the garden, his back to her. He was wearing jeans and a pale blue denim work shirt, sleeves shoved carelessly past his elbows, and she could see the corded muscles along his tanned forearms tighten as he gripped the windowframe.

Kailin swallowed as she watched him move away from the window and resume his slow circuit of the table, working his way casually yet deliberately toward her. Somehow she'd been hoping that something would have defused that restless tension within him, but it was still there, as volatile as ever. Her heart sank. Time hadn't mellowed Brett Douglass; it had just seasoned him.

A hundred trite phrases ran through her mind. She discarded all of them and simply stood in silence, letting those wary blue eyes search hers, seeking God knew what. *What can I say?* she asked him silently. *Oh, Brett, what can I say that will erase the hurt and anger and suspicion?*

He stopped finally just a few feet from her and stood there with his hands on his hips, letting his eyes wander over her. Kailin could have screamed, but she managed to stand absolutely still. His gaze moved from her high-heeled sandals, up the narrow linen skirt with its expensive leather belt, the silk leopard-print blouse with the simple gold chain at the open throat, the flamboyant wood-and-feather earrings. Not quite the antiestablishment jeans and T-shirts the Kailin Yarbro of the past had favored. His eyes paused on her shoulder-length hair, still casual but less tousled. She nearly smiled in spite of her nervousness. What had he expected? Banker's gray with a dress-for-success bow at the throat? Cashmere and pearls?

"Eleven years older and wiser, Brett," she found herself saying. "Other than that, everything's about the same."

His eyes met hers for an instant. Then they crinkled slightly at the outer corners, and he smiled. "Sorry."

"Don't be." She returned the smile. "You're not quite the young college rebel I remember, either. What happened to the earring and the beard?"

"I grew up."

"So did I." Check and countercheck.

He nodded slowly, that speculative gaze running over her again. Then his eyes focused on hers. "You're looking damned good, Kailin. It's been a long time."

"Yes." *Too long*. The silence pulled taut between them, and finally Kailin couldn't stand it. Decisively she walked the few steps between them. He watched her warily as she put her hands lightly on his forearms for balance and stood on tiptoe, lifting her mouth to his cheek. She could have sworn he flinched as her lips brushed his skin. "I'm glad to see you again, Brett."

He didn't say a word. They stood like that for a long while, so close that she could see the small crescent-shaped scar on his jaw that was a souvenir from a flying bottle during a demonstration against something she couldn't even remember now. She expected him to kiss her back. But he simply stared down at her, eyes cool and expressionless. Then he stepped carefully away, leaving her standing there feeling silly.

A jolt of sudden anger ran through Kailin. In all the hours she'd spent torturing herself over Brett's possible reactions, she'd never once anticipated such remoteness, such... hostility. It was as though he held *her* responsible for everything that had happened. *He* was the one who had spurned her; *he* was the one who had run off without even trying to find out the truth, who had left her to grieve for their lost child among strangers.

Her instinctive reaction was to snap back at him, but she restrained herself and instead said calmly, "Look, Brett, I know my turning up here without any warning is a shock. I should have called you first. Warned you. But—" She caught herself awkwardly. Why *hadn't* she called him? She didn't really know herself, except that she'd been afraid. "We...I... Oh, hell!" She ran her fingers through her hair, combing it back from her face impatiently. "This is all so complicated and...messy."

"Messy?" He shot her a narrow-eyed look, anger etched in every line on his face. "Is that what you think this is, Kailin? Messy?"

Oh, God, she thought despairingly, is this what it's going to be like? "More than messy, I guess," she said quietly, trying to mollify him and hating herself for it. "Awkward was the word I was looking for. I'd accepted this job before I knew you were down here. When I found out, it was too late. I'd already agreed to do it, and I couldn't just back out because of—"

"Because of me?" Bitterness ran through the words, hot as bile.

"Brett—" She caught herself, hearing the anger in her own voice and refusing to give in to it. She took a deep breath and tried again. "Brett, I know I've caught you by surprise. I'm sorry if I...if I've upset you. I'd hoped we could be friends, but if we can't be that much, can we at least be civil to each other? It's going to be very difficult working together if we can't . . . talk.''

"We never *did* talk much," he retorted, eyes and mouth hard and unyielding. "We were always in so much of a hurry to get into bed we never had much time for anything else."

It was the truth, but the way he said it made Kailin wince. "You make it sound so cheap," she whispered. "As though there was nothing more than—"

"Sex?" he shot back. "Sex was all we ever had. Raw and wild and plenty of it. You knew exactly what you wanted, and you took it. We both did. But we're grown-up now. Let's not pretend we ever had anything else."

Kailin stared at him in disbelief. "You can't possibly believe that," she said raggedly. "Brett, how can you—?''

"There's something I've always wondered about, Kailin," he said with a savage smile, settling one solid shoulder against the windowframe as he turned to face her. "How did good old Royce enjoy being second?"

For an instant Kailin felt so light-headed that she wondered if she'd fainted. The room spun gently around her until all she could see was Brett's face looming over her, his eyes hard and cold and bitter. "What?" she finally managed to whisper as the room wobbled to a stop. "What did you say?"

"Royce," he repeated with a sharklike smile. "You remember him, don't you, Kailin? Your husband?''

"I—"

"Did he ever ask you what it had been like with me, Kailin?" His voice was low now, a soft wash of intimate sound that excluded everything but the two of them. "Did he ever ask how he rated? I'll bet it galled the hell out of him, didn't it, knowing I'd been there before him." The savage smile widened. "Did he know I'd been your first, Kailin? Did he know that every damn thing you knew about making love was what I'd taught you?''

"Brett!" It was no more than a cry of pain. Kailin felt herself sway and snatched the edge of the table to keep from falling.

"I used to think about the two of you together," he went on in that low, harsh voice. "I used to lie awake at night wanting you so badly my whole body ached with it, and I used to think of you making love with him."

"Brett, for the love of God!" She spun away from him with a cry of anguish. She squeezed her eyes shut, trying to blot out the memories, trying not to listen.

"When he's making love to you, Kailin, do you ever think of me?" He sounded closer now, his voice a slash of anger. "Do you ever wish it was me there beside you instead of him? Do you ever whisper my name in his ear when you're whispering all those other little things, and at the end is it ever my name you cry instead of his?"

"Stop it!" Kailin clamped her hands over her ears, feeling hot tears well up and not caring.

"Or does he even take you that far, Kailin?" that soft, purring voice went on relentlessly. "Or does he leave you alone with your memories, wanting me even half as badly as I've wanted you all these years?"

"Stop it!" Kailin's voice rose in an anguished sob. "Brett, stop it! Why are you doing this to me?"

"Because I want to see you hurt like I've hurt!"

He said it with such ragged savagery, the words so shocking in their honesty, that Kailin knew they had been torn out of him before he'd even given them thought.

"Tit for tat, lady," he growled, sounding subdued now, as though his own reply had shocked him out of his anger.

"Oh, Brett," she whispered raggedly, turning to look at him. "I never meant to hurt you. I loved you."

"Love!" His face was white and drawn, his eyes dark with some old pain she could only guess at. "You used me, Kailin, but you never loved me. You didn't even know what love was. You used to flaunt me at those parties like I was some damned Gypsy, knowing it was like dropping a spark into gasoline. And you used me to drive your father crazy, because I was the best weapon you had. You loved the excitement I brought into your life, Kailin. You loved the danger and you loved playing at rebellion, but you didn't love me. I wasn't good enough for you, remember? Quentin J. Yarbro's high-society daughter could take a roll in the hay with a country vet's son, but she sure as hell wasn't going to marry him. *That* honor went to one of the local rich boys."

"Brett, that wasn't how it was! Yes, I used you to annoy my father—I was nineteen, and I was rich and spoiled and used to getting my own way. I'm not proud of that, but I can't change what I was. But you used me, too, remember. All you talked about that entire summer was how much it must be driving Quentin J. Yarbro crazy knowing his daughter was dating the man responsible for picketing Yarbro Paint and Chemicals. We used each other, Brett, don't kid yourself about that. But I loved you. And never once during that entire summer did you ever give me one sign that you loved me back."

He was staring at her, a muscle along his jawline throbbing as though he had his teeth clenched. His eyes were dark and disbelieving, and Kailin felt something start to ache within her. "When I went to your apartment that night and told you I was pregnant, you laughed at me. And later, when I got home, my father told me he'd offered you ten thousand dollars if you'd leave me. He said you'd taken it. I knew you needed the money badly for school. I . . ." She dropped her gaze. "I believed him. After all the things you said, I had no reason not to. I . . . I was hurting. Can't you understand that?"

"Yeah, I can understand hurt," he said in a ragged voice. "And that's why you married McGuire?"

She nodded, not trusting her voice.

"You weren't lying that night when you came to see me, were you?" he asked suddenly, quietly. "About the baby."

"No." There was a taut silence, broken only by the clatter of palm fronds in the wind.

Did he know what had happened? she wondered. Did he know about the miscarriage that had cost him his unborn child? She had her mouth half-open, wanting to ask, then subsided again with an inward sigh. It didn't matter now. Telling him the truth would only hurt him more than he was already hurting. She frowned as the familiar pain ran through her. Strange how she could grieve so long over a baby she'd never even known. She knew it was because it had been Brett's. It wasn't really the death of her unborn child she was still grieving, it was the death of love.

She looked up to find Brett staring down at her, his eyes dark and wistful. Although he didn't move, he seemed to reach toward her, his gaze caressing her face like the touch of a loving hand. "We could have had it all, Kailin," he whispered. "I loved you so much it hurts just to think about it. But you threw it all away."

"You never told me." She spoke softly. It was such a simple thing when it was said aloud. "You never once said that, Brett. Never once."

Something like pain flickered across his features. He frowned and looked down. "Yeah," he said. "I guess you're right. Somehow I thought that if you loved someone enough you didn't have to say anything."

"We were both such kids." She sighed and scooped her hair off her face again, feeling worn-out and empty. "Too scared to say 'I love you' out loud, in case we made fools of ourselves."

"Are you happy, Kailin?"

The question surprised her so much that she simply stared at him. Then she laughed quietly and nodded. "Yes, Brett. I am. Very happy."

Again, some emotion she couldn't identify flickered across his features. He nodded abruptly, then turned away and walked across the room.

"And you?"

He paused in the process of pulling a chair away from the table and looked up at her. Then he smiled. It was a grim little smile that scarcely moved his lips. "Does it matter?"

"Brett—" Something moved in the corner of her eye. Kailin glanced toward the door, then swallowed what she'd been about to say with an inward sigh, hoping she didn't look even half as rattled as she felt.

"Hi, gorgeous." Craig Bryant sauntered into the room with just the right amount of nonchalance, his hands shoved into the pockets of his fashionably baggy slacks. He grinned winningly at her. "No one else here yet?"

"Mr. Douglass is here," she replied coolly, taking the rest of the papers from her portfolio and setting them on the table.

Craig saw Brett at the precise instant Kailin said it. The smile dropped from his mouth, and he eyed the other man with open dislike. "Thought you'd be out organizing a rally or something, Douglass. I hear your little group's out to ban bug repellent next. If you pull it off, it'll be a great winter—we'll all be too busy swatting mosquitoes to worry about Paradise Point. Or is that the idea?"

The sarcasm didn't seem to faze Brett. He smiled lazily and tilted the chair onto its back legs. "Hadn't thought of that, but now that you mention it . . ." He grinned, obviously enjoying baiting Craig. "And we'd win, Bryant. They've been spraying Florida wetlands with insecticide for years to cut down on the mosquito problem. All they've managed to do is contaminate the marshes so badly half the bird and gator eggs laid each season don't hatch, and you wouldn't recognize some of the things that come out of the ones that do. And the animals aren't the only things suffering out there—people are fed up with being poisoned, having their kids sick all the time—''

Craig made a noise in his throat. ''You guys jump on any bandwagon that comes along. Last year it was nuclear power plants, year before that chemical waste, before *that* whales and seals. Next you'll be trying to fence off the entire state of Florida and turn it into a natural habitat.''

''We've thought of that,'' Brett replied agreeably. ''Maybe next year. *This* year we're after you, Bryant—and all the other money-grubbing land developers who think they can break the rules and not get caught.'' His smile reminded Kailin of a cruising barracuda. ''You're not getting away with it, Bryant, old buddy. Not this time.''

''Damn you, Douglass, I'll—''

''Excuse me, gentlemen,'' Kailin said smoothly, ''but perhaps we can save the accusations and name-calling for later?'' For some reason she found it solidly reassuring to find that Brett hadn't changed that much after all. Still fighting the good fight. She smiled, more to herself than at the two men who were still trading looks across the wide table. ''Is anyone else from Gulf Coast Development attending this meeting, Mr. Bryant?''

''I'm here alone.'' He smiled warmly. ''And it's Craig, remember?''

''Break your leash, Bryant?'' Brett asked lazily.

''And just what the hell does that mean?''

''Last I heard, you were halfway to being a married man. Or did your fiancée see the light and toss you out?''

Kailin held her breath for an instant, certain that Craig was going to launch himself across the table at Brett, but at the last moment he managed to restrain himself. He flexed his shoulders and sat down, nostrils flared. ''Coming from a man who's bedded every single woman and half the married ones within a hundred-mile radius, that doesn't deserve an answer.''

Brett's features darkened, but to Kailin's relief, he maintained a hostile silence.

Terrific start, Kailin thought to herself, trying to ignore the little twinge that Craig's accusations sent through her. It wasn't any of her business if Brett *had* slept with every woman in Florida, or if he planned to work his way north, state by state. She slipped Brett a sidelong glance, but he was staring over Craig's shoulder at the window, where the first streaks of rain were hitting.

She was saved from further thoughts of Brett's alleged sexual activities by an explosion of activity at the door. A group of people herded through, flapping wet raincoats and umbrellas in a spray of water, all chattering and exclaiming at once. There was an abrupt silence when they saw her. Then they hastily made their way around the table, glancing curiously at her as they trooped by.

"I'm Kailin McGuire," she said quietly when they'd settled themselves and fallen more or less silent. "And I'm sorry for calling you out in this weather." She glanced at the window as a crash of thunder rattled the frame. "I'm used to blizzards at this time of year, not hurricanes." There was a spate of laughter, and she felt the tension in the room ease.

"This isn't a hurricane, Ms. McGuire," one of the men drawled. He shifted the dead cigar from one corner of his mouth to the other. "A hurricane's when the roof lifts off. This is just a dust-settler."

Another crash of thunder punctuated his sentence, and a deluge of rain hit the window like a blow from a fist. Kailin winced. "I'll take your word for that, Mr. ...Cheevers, isn't it? I spoke with you on the phone yesterday."

"That's right." The cigar shifted again. "And before we get started, ma'am, I'd like to know just what side you're on here."

"I'm not on anyone's side. My job is to mediate an agreement between you—the Barrier Islands Land Use Committee—and Gulf Coast Development on the Paradise

Point resort complex. It's true that I was hired by the private investors backing Paradise Point, but I assure you that your best interests and theirs are *not* mutually exclusive.''

Cheevers gave a disbelieving grunt. ''Frankly, ma'am, I think you're wasting your time. They—'' he nodded in Craig's direction ''—aren't interest in anything but getting that complex finished, no matter how many laws they have to break getting there.''

Craig leaped to his feet, pointing an accusing finger at his opponent. ''And you and your committee won't rest until you bankrupt us and turn Paradise Point into a bird preserve!''

''Gentlemen,'' Kailin interjected smoothly, ''this isn't going to get us anywhere. Shall we all sit down?'' Calmly, with a firmness born of experience, Kailin waited until Craig sat down. ''I've ordered coffee and a selection of pastries, but I'd like to get started. We have a lot of ground to cover this afternoon, and the sooner we get down to it, the sooner we can discover where we all stand.'' It took an effort, but Kailin looked down the table at Brett. ''I know you're chairman of the Land Use Committee, Mr. Douglass, but I haven't met the others yet. Perhaps you could introduce me, then we can get down to work.''

He was watching her with an odd expression on his face, and he nodded slowly, leaving Kailin wondering what he'd been thinking. Just what, she mused, did he think of finding her here playing establishment executive when the last time he'd seen her she'd been scathing in her criticism of that same establishment? Of course, she reminded herself with amusement, he'd obviously learned to play the games himself, using homegrown political pressure groups to accomplish what marches and pickets had. Old rebels don't die, she thought with an inward smile, they just grow up, don three-piece suits and gnaw away at the system from the inside.

After the introductions had been made, Brett leaned well back in the chair and laced his hands behind his head. "Okay, Ms. McGuire," he said with a challenging stare. "It's your show now."

She was good, Brett had to admit a few minutes later. She was damned good!

He watched Kailin speculatively and found himself trying to equate this articulate businesswoman with the temperamental teenager he'd known in Greenlake. It didn't seem possible that she could be the same woman, yet there was no mistaking that funny little leap his heart gave every time their eyes met. God, what was the matter with him? Eleven years and a broken heart later, and she could still make his blood race with just a single glance.

You're a damned fool, he told himself bluntly. He thought of the whirlwind of emotion that had torn through him when he'd walked through the door and realized that in that instant he'd nearly thrown away all his best intentions. He'd approached her, absorbed by the reality of her, drawing the warm, oddly erotic scent of her deep into his lungs as a cigarette addict draws in nicotine. Time had gone spinning away and he'd felt caught in a strange mélange of past and present, and for one heartbeat he'd put his hand out to swing her into his arms.

But he hadn't. Strength, he wondered now, or cowardice? They sometimes got as tangled and confused as love and hate, and it was often just as hard to tell one from the other.

Involuntarily he thought of his outburst only moments later. The rage and pain must have been festering inside him for eleven years. Now he found he didn't feel much of anything. He found himself watching Kailin with a dispassionate curiosity. And that, he decided, was almost worse than hating her.

She had them eating out of her hands, Brett realized with surprise. They'd all come in here convinced that she was the enemy, and within ten minutes she'd defused the tension and suspicion with the skill of a seasoned diplomat.

He found himself watching her with growing admiration, drinking in her soft, musical voice as she spoke with authority and self-confidence, the graceful gestures of her slender hands, the intent tilt of her head when she was listening to someone. Framed by softly waving hair, her features seemed stronger and more defined. Her eyes were still vividly green, but when they occasionally, briefly brushed his, he could see a seriousness that had never been there before. Kailin McGuire had grown up.

They both had. Brett eased his breath out in a quiet sigh that felt suspiciously like regret. He frowned. Douglass, he told himself fiercely, don't you get caught in her web again. She might have grown up, but she hasn't changed. No one changes that much.

He realized that she was watching him with an odd expression on her face, as though she knew exactly what he was thinking. For an instant he thought he saw something like sadness brush her features. Then it was gone.

Damn it, why was he tied up in knots while she was as cool as a cucumber? Twenty minutes ago she'd been in tears, and to look at her now you'd think she'd never set eyes on him before. It had always driven him nuts, that ability she had to close out things she didn't want to deal with.

If you think you're going to shut me out that easily, Kailin McGuire, he thought, you're making a big mistake. I don't know why you're down here, but it isn't half as innocent as you'd have us all believe. You're not Quentin J. Yarbro's daughter for nothing. But you're on *my* turf now. So whatever the hell you're up to, I'm going to find out what it is.

"Can we cut through the bull and get to the bottom line, Ms. McGuire?" he heard himself say suddenly. In the startled silence that followed, Brett felt all eyes swing his way. But he was aware only of the pair locked with his, green as grass and narrowed.

Three

<hr>

And what bottom line would that be, Mr. Douglass?"

Kailin spoke casually, easily, but her look held a trace of weariness, and Brett felt a sense of satisfaction at having gotten even that small a reaction. "You know the bottom line I mean, Ms. McGuire. The one with the dollars and cents on it."

Her eyes narrowed again, almost imperceptibly. "If you mean the costs involved with canceling the Paradise Point project outright, they're in the report by your left elbow. If you're referring to the estimates to repair the storm damage on Phase Two and the updated figures from Phase Three construction, they're in the one by your *right* elbow." She emphasized the word slightly, just enough to let him know that she was perfectly aware he hadn't been listening to a thing she'd been saying.

"But as I've already said, Mr. Douglass, those figures are all based on projections done by Gulf Coast Development *prior* to my involvement. They're going to be very different once we've established a new plan of attack." She smiled faintly. "But since we have yet to work up such a plan, I have no way of knowing yet what the 'bottom line,' as you put it, will be."

Brett smiled back. "I have a feeling, Ms. McGuire, that you've not only figured out a plan of attack but have the cost worked out to the last penny. All that remains is to convince us that we thought it up ourselves, then cajole us into signing the papers giving Gulf Coast Development approval to start construction on Phase Three of Paradise Point."

A flicker of something—worry, anger, apprehension—darkened Kailin's eyes for an instant, then vanished. She still seemed calm and in control, but she'd gone very still. "Mr. Douglass," she said after a moment, "I'm here at the request of the investors who put up the money for the resort. Obviously it would be in their best interests for the entire resort to be completed and sold out. It would also," she added with a hint of impatience in her voice, "be in Sanibel Island's best interests.

"You depend heavily on tourism down here. The Paradise Point condominiums are top-of-the-line—they'll bring not only solid tax revenue to the community, but the support industries on the island such as restaurants, recreation and so on will also benefit. What we're trying to do here is come up with a workable compromise to attain that end. I'm not trying to *cajole* anyone into anything."

Brett leaned back in his chair and propped his foot on the leg of the table, draping his arm over his upraised knee. "You want us to approve Phase Three," he said flatly, giving her no way out.

"Yes."

It surprised him. He'd expected an argument, or at the very least a circuitous reply designed to sound like one thing while meaning something else altogether. For some reason her honesty irritated him. "The Land Use Committee has withheld approval for start of construction on Phase Three," he said in the slow and elaborately patient voice of a parent explaining something to a small child, "because Gulf Coast made a hash out of Phase Two."

"That's crazy, Douglass," Craig Bryant snapped. "Phrase Two had its problems during construction, we've admitted that. But you can't blame that storm last week on us!"

"Blame, hell!" Brett growled. "It was the best thing that's happened to Sanibel in years. If it hadn't blown down most of those cardboard boxes you called condos we'd never have known just *how* badly they'd been built in the first place." He leaned forward slightly. "You're just lucky that no one was living in them when that storm hit, Bryant, or I'd have had you up on murder charges."

"That's getting pretty damned close to libel."

"Sue me."

"Gentlemen, please."

Brett eased his weight back into his chair and swung his gaze onto Kailin. "Six years ago, when we gave Gulf Coast the green light to build Paradise Point, Charlie Bryant was still president of the corporation. Our agreement was with him, and with the way he did business. He was in charge when Phase One was finished a year ago, and it not only met our requirements, it surpassed them."

Brett paused long enough to give Craig a slow stare. "Then Charlie stepped down, and his son took over." He could see a slow flush of anger rise from the throat of Craig's shirt. "In the last year, Gulf Coast Development has gone from being one of the most respected land development firms in this country to a national joke." Brett looked at Kailin again, ignoring an inarticulate sputter from Craig. "Investors have been bailing out like rats off a sinking ship, leaving Gulf Coast so tight for cash they're selling land they don't even own yet just to raise the weekly payroll. Their operating capital's down to nothing. They built Phase Two out of cobwebs and spit, praying it held together long enough for the units to sell so they'd have collateral to finance Phase Three. But Phase Two's nothing but kindling after last week's storm. They're going to have to bulldoze the site clean and start from scratch.''

"That," snarled Craig, "is a damned lie! Sure it sustained some storm damage—hell, half the houses on the island were damaged. But not one person who's put down a deposit has asked for his money back. The only thing that's going to keep Phase Two from selling out is this committee's refusal to approve Phase Three. You all know that Phase Three includes the recreation and marina facilities for the whole resort—without the airstrip, the golf course and docking facilities, you've undercut the main selling feature of the whole complex. *That's* why we haven't sold Phase Two out—because of the uncertainty you people have created with all this foot-dragging! People aren't willing to risk buying a unit in Paradise Point only to have a bunch of small-town loonies renege on its original agreement and—"

"Now wait a minute!" Dorothy Enright sat bolt upright, eyes widening in indignation. "You can't—"

"Ladies and gentlemen! Please!"

"Our original agreement with Gulf Coast granted approval for Phase Three *if* this committee was satisfied that the terms of the original agreement were met on Phases One and Two. And you haven't even come close.''

"May I remind you all," Kailin interrupted in a precise voice, "that this meeting was called to ascertain where both parties presently stand—*not* to lay blame for past mistakes.''

There was a startled silence, and even Brett found himself wincing slightly at the impatience in her voice.

Kailin let her cool stare move from face to face. "Nobody wants to see Paradise Point fold. The investors and Gulf Coast for obvious reasons, the people presently living in Phase One and those who have purchased units in Phase Two for even *more* obvious reasons—and this committee. It's as much in Sanibel's favor to see this resort built and sold out as it is everyone else's. If Gulf Coast goes bankrupt, you're going to be stuck with a half-completed resort complex that'll be hung up in court for years.''

Again that steady, appraising gaze moved around the table. ''And I mean *years*. It could be a decade or more before you can resell the land, and in the meantime Phase One will steadily deteriorate, the owners will dump their units onto the market for whatever they can get, and you're going to have nothing out there but a ghost town. Land on Sanibel is too precious for that. I know it, you know it, and Gulf Coast knows it. So instead of trying to outshout each other why don't we discuss how to best satisfy *everyone's* needs?''

''I'd like to know what Gulf Coast has to say,'' Dorothy Enright said. She was a tall, lean woman with short steel-colored hair and a mind like a bear trap. ''Mr. Bryant has been uncharacteristically quiet so far.''

Brett could have sworn that Craig Bryant winced.

''There...have been some changes at Gulf Coast,'' Kailin said quietly. She glanced at Craig as though waiting for him to say something, but he remained sullenly silent, and Brett sat up, suddenly interested. ''Mr. Bryant is here in an advisory capacity only,'' she said quietly. ''Until further notice all business transactions will be handled by a board of directors, upon the request of Mr. Charles Bryant.''

There was a moment of stunned silence as everyone assessed the implications of Craig's removal. Then the group started talking at once. Kailin held up her hand for silence. ''I'm sorry, but I can't tell you any more. However, I will be dealing directly with Charles Bryant—and so will this committee.

''Gulf Coast is *very* serious about reaching a workable solution on Paradise Point,'' Kailin said into an attentive silence. ''This move was made at the recommendation of the investors." She paused delicately. "At my recommendation, actually. Part of Gulf Coast's difficulties seemed to be caused by personality conflicts and certain . . . management practices. Mr. Bryant Senior agreed that the first step lay in alleviating those problems."

Brett felt his grudging admiration for her take another leap. He had no doubt that Charlie's return to the fray was at Kailin's instigation. Replace Bryant junior or face foreclosure, he imagined her saying and smiled. Even though he didn't trust Kailin McGuire, he certainly had to admire her tactics.

"I've spent the past month assessing this situation," Kailin was saying quietly. "For those of you who don't already know, that's what I do for a living. I'm an industrial troubleshooter. Companies that are in serious trouble hire me to come in and figure out why. And, with luck, get them out of it. The Board of Directors has offered me its complete cooperation. That means," she emphasized, looking around the table, "that they are open to negotiation."

"What kind of negotiation?" Dorothy asked. "And how open?"

"Gulf Coast Development is teetering on the edge of bankruptcy," she said bluntly, ignoring the gasps of surprise. "Paradise Point is the only major project that Gulf Coast has under way, and, quite simply, it's going to make or break the company."

"Holy cats," John Grohman muttered, looking mildly horrified. "Do you mean that we're holding the trump card?"

"That's exactly what I mean," Kailin said. "And since I'm confident that no one here wants to see Gulf Coast file for bankruptcy—if for no other reason than the problems it will create for your community—you can see why it's important that we work together."

"You said you'd reviewed the situation," Peter Rylie said suddenly. "Do you have any recommendations?"

"I have a few ideas," Kailin assured him with a smile. "But I'd rather not discuss them until you've all had an opportunity to think over what I've said and to read the material in those two reports. I *am* confident, though, that we can come to some mutually satisfying agreement."

Mutually satisfying. The phrase made Brett smile involuntarily as he found himself thinking of the last time he'd heard her use it. "It's been a most satisfactory afternoon," she'd purred as she'd been leaving. "Satisfying, too. Mutually satisfying, don't you agree?"

Brett's smile widened. He'd agreed, no doubt about it. There hadn't been an afternoon before or since that had come even close to the magic they'd shared that day.

Kailin's eyes happened to meet his just then, and he knew in that instant that she, too, was reminded of that lazy Sunday. They'd spent their time in what had been one deliciously prolonged afternoon of lovemaking—they would fall asleep, his body still a part of hers, then awaken an hour or so later and start over again. It took no effort at all to remember the hot, musky scent of the rumpled sheets, the sensual feel of Kailin's love-damp skin against his, the soft catch in her voice next to his ear as she begged him for *more....*

God! Brett dragged his eyes from hers with a physical effort, feeling his heart racing. He closed his eyes, praying no one else in the room had heard the groan that had escaped. He felt hot and dizzy and realized without surprise that he was vitally and painfully aroused.

He took a deep breath, furious with himself for being so weak. It had been eleven years. Eleven *years*!

Even if he wanted her, he couldn't have her. She belonged to Royce McGuire. She'd always belonged to Royce McGuire. That summer-long romp with him had been nothing more than a rich girl's whim.

He forced himself to look at Kailin, but she steadfastly refused to meet his eyes. Good, he thought with a flash of uncharacteristically malicious satisfaction. Maybe she wasn't quite as immune to the past as she was letting on. Maybe she hadn't quite forgotten *everything*....

"...meet and go over these reports," a voice at his elbow was saying.

Brett blinked and stared at John Grohman. He looked at the two colored folders in John's hands, then around the room, and realized that the meeting was over.

"You with us at all today, Douglass?" Zac asked testily. He eyed Brett impatiently, gnawing on his dead cigar. "If I didn't know better, I'd say you were in love."

"What?" Brett frowned, then shook his head to dispel the shadows of the past. "Sorry, I was just thinking about Gulf Coast," he lied. "Let's go over those tomorrow, okay? We don't have to waste much time—it's obvious what they want." When the two men stared at him blankly, he dismissed the reports with a flip of his hand. "They want us to green-light Phase Three without even a whimper."

"Now, Brett," John protested, "I didn't get that impression at all. Gulf Coast has its back to the wall; if anyone's going to be giving concessions, it's them. And with old Charlie back in the saddle..."

Zac grunted. "You know I've been dead set against Phase Three right from the beginning, Douglass, but I think John's got a point there. I figure we can get everything we want if we play our hand right."

Brett stood up impatiently. "Take my word for it, you two—Gulf Coast isn't going to give up a damned thing. They want compromises, for sure, but they want *us* to do the compromising."

"But with this mediator sitting—"

"This mediator," Brett interrupted brusquely, "isn't anything more than a pretty smoke screen. She's sitting squarely in Gulf Coast's backyard, and she's going to be pressuring us all the way."

"Brett, I usually agree with you, but this time I think you're wrong." Dorothy Enright's piercing gray gaze held his. "I don't know what this woman has done to get your back up, but you're not thinking straight on this one—not with your brains, anyway." Her mouth twitched in what, by Dorothy, passed for a smile. "Leave your male hormones out of this, Douglass. It's too important." With that she turned on one heel and strode to the door, looking every inch the former sergeant major she was.

"Damn it," Brett breathed, glaring at the other two. "Is that what you think, too?"

Zac grinned. "I think you've changed your tune pretty fast, that's all. Yesterday you were trying to push me into voting for approval, today you're dead set against it." The cigar shifted. "She's a mighty attractive woman, Douglass."

"So was Mata Hari," Brett muttered. He shoved past Zac and headed for the door, still rankled by Dorothy's gibe. It wasn't hormones talking where Kailin was concerned, it was common sense. And experience. Plenty of experience!

Zac Cheevers's law offices were in the top level of a two-story shopping complex surrounded by tropical gardens. A roofed walkway ran the perimeter of the upper level, its protected wooden railing draped with flowering vines.

Kailin paused at the top of the long flight of wooden steps leading down to the parking lot and drew in a deep breath of clean, wet air. The storm had passed. The crushed-coral-and-shell parking lot glinted with puddles of rainwater, and the air held a welcome freshness. She turned her face gratefully to the sun streaming down through a patchwork of puffy clouds and concentrated on relaxing the muscles knotted across her shoulders.

That meeting was step one. It was always the hardest because it required breaking through everyone's suspicion and anger. That was the problem with a job like hers: she was called in only after everything else had failed, when tempers were raw and antagonisms deeply embedded. It was like walking through a mine field.

"That was an impressive bit of work in there, Ms. McGuire."

Kailin wasn't particularly surprised when the quiet male voice broke through her reverie. Perhaps, she thought idly as she turned to look at him, that was why she'd dawdled out here in the first place. "Thank you, Mr. Douglass. You were fairly impressive yourself. Do you and Craig Bryant always get along so well?"

"Bryant's a jerk," Brett retorted flatly. He strolled to the porch railing and sat on it, hitching one leg up. "He's greedy, he's ambitious, and in the year and a half since he's taken over Gulf Coast he's damned near run it into the ground." He smiled and gave her an appraising look. "Of course, you know all that. You were the one who got him turfed out." When she didn't deny it, his eyes narrowed slightly. "You reminded me of your father up there today."

"Somehow I don't think you meant that as a compliment."

"I didn't."

Kailin watched him in frowning silence. He was like a tropical storm himself, all brooding shadows and thunderheads. Just what did he expect from her, anyway?

"How *is* your father?"

"Not . . . too well." Where was *this* leading? "He had a heart attack about six months ago."

"I didn't think he had one." There was an awkward pause, then Brett sighed and ran his fingers through his hair. "Damn it, that was a stupid thing to say. I'm sorry."

Kailin laughed quietly. "Don't be. It was just as much a shock to everyone who'd ever known him—a bigger shock to him. I think he was disappointed in a way. I know he was furious that his body dared betray him like that. He was like a bear for weeks, making everyone's life more miserable than usual.''

Brett looked around at her, a hint of a smile warming his firm mouth. "I can't see Quentin J. Yarbro being an invalid for long. He probably just *ordered* his heart to repair itself and was back to his usual rampaging self in a week.''

''What it did was scare him. For the first time in my life I actually saw my father faced with something he couldn't control—and it terrified him. He hasn't been the same since." She frowned and looked out across the shimmering parking lot. A tiny green lizard scampered up one of the railing supports into the sun. It paused there to soak up the warmth, glistening like cut emeralds.

She felt awkward and uneasy, afraid of saying something that would set off another outburst like his earlier one. She'd planned all the the things she would say if she ever saw him again, but they all seemed futile and empty.

She shook off her moodiness and looked up to find Brett watching her. Their eyes met and held, and for a breathless eternity Kailin stood riveted there. One step, something whispered coaxingly. Just one step, and you'll be in his arms again....

She turned away instead, angry and confused at how easily she could still make a fool of herself over this man.

"Gulf Coast is fighting for its life."

The brusque change of topic knocked her off balance for a moment. Then she recovered, wondering if he'd seen a hint of that weakness in her eyes. "Yes." She strolled to the railing and leaned against it, lifting her face to the sun again.

"Are you paid a percentage of future profit if you succeed in pulling it through?"

"I don't get a percentage of anything," she replied quietly. "I'm paid a flat fee, win or lose. But I like to win. Call it old-fashioned pride if you like, but I love catching a failing company at the brink of ruin and helping it struggle back onto its feet."

"And if we don't approve Phase Three?"

"Gulf Coast will go bankrupt, the investors will lose everything they've put into it, and Sanibel Island will be stuck with a white elephant called Paradise Point." She smiled. "It's a classic no-win situation, Mr. Chairman. I'd really suggest you approve Phrase Three."

"That sounds like a threat."

"For God's sake, Brett!" Kailin fought her impatience and lost badly. "I know you, remember—you're a realist. You know as well as I do that sooner or later *someone* is going to develop that land. You've been pushing for approval for the past six months, so you're as aware as I am of the problems you're facing if Gulf Coast fails."

"Sure the Point's going to be developed—but it has to be the right people doing it. That leaves Craig Bryant out. His father did a good job, but Craig's dangerous, Kailin. Phase Two is nothing but rubble after that storm. If we allow him to rebuild—and give him approval to start building Phase Three—he's not going to put up anything better. And I'm damned if I'm going to have the lives of innocent people on my conscience when the whole mess blows into the sea!"

"My reports on the storm damage don't indicate anything nearly as bad as you keep telling me."

"*Your* reports? Or Craig Bryant's reports?" When Kailin remained silent, Brett nodded. "I thought so. He's feeding you what he wants you to know, Kailin. Have you been out to the Point yet?"

"No," Kailin admitted. "The road is...apparently closed."

"I'll just bet it is."

"How do you know what the damage is?"

"I went in by boat a couple of days and looked, that's how."

"Well, I'm not going to work up my recommendations until I've seen it, too, so don't worry." She smiled at him dryly. "I'm not supposed to be taking sides here, but I'll give you a piece of free advice— Charlie Bryant wants to save his company. Play your cards right and you can get every concession you've ever wanted out of them.''

"And what concessions do *you* want, Kailin?" He looked at her coolly. "That's the real bottom line I'm interested in hearing about. Just what is Kailin McGuire getting out of this?''

The bitterness in Brett's voice made Kailin look at him sharply.

"McGuire International is into real estate, isn't it?"

Kailin found herself staring stupidly at him while she mentally scrambled to follow another unexpected shift in the conversation. "Yes, I think so. I know they have holdings in the Caribbean and Mexico—hotels, I think.''

"You think.''

Kailin turned until she was facing him squarely, fighting a little frisson of anger. "Brett, I'm getting damned tired of this. If you're trying to say something, spit it out. I don't like playing games.''

"No?" He gave a bark of raw laughter. "Hell, Kailin, you *invented* game playing." Then, abruptly, he sobered. "But you're right, let's be frank. McGuire International owns eight major European hotels, two Caribbean resorts and a combined health spa and tennis clinic just outside Mexico City.''

She saw where he was headed. "Brett..." she started warningly.

"Do you think I can't see what's going on?" he said angrily. "Gulf Coast is on the rocks, a prime takeover target, and McGuire International wants it. But they're not interested in acquiring it while the Paradise Point project is still up in the air. They sent you down here to soften us up—*me* up. You said it yourself—you know me. You know how my mind works. What better person to send down than someone who knows her opponent, right?''

"Don't be absurd!" His accusations were so preposterous that Kailin didn't know whether to laugh or cry. "Listen to yourself Brett, you've turned paranoia into an art form!"

"Did Royce put you up to this, or was it your idea?" he asked belligerently. "How *is* old Royce these days?"

Kailin stared at him. Oh God, she thought, shocked, he doesn't know! "Brett, there's something you—"

"Just what has your husband got riding on this, anyway?"

Without warning, Kailin's patience evaporated. "My husband is dead."

Brett blinked, then stared at her in stunned silence.

"Royce was killed in a car accident nearly six years ago. Which has nothing to do with this, anyway, because I have never had anything to do with *any* aspect of the McGuire business, before *or* after Royce's death."

"Oh, Kailin." Brett drew in a deep, unsteady breath. He'd gone pale and was staring at her, his eyes dark with shock. "I...those things I said earlier," he whispered hoarsely. "About the two of you. I...damn it!" A flush suffused his face, and he wheeled away from her, swearing softly. "Kailin, I'm sorry. I was trying to hurt you, but I never dreamed..."

To her surprise, Kailin felt her sudden hot anger melt away. She gazed at Brett's back, wondering why seeing him squirm gave her no satisfaction at all. She should have been rejoicing at making him pay for the things he'd said, but for some reason she found herself feeling badly for his obvious discomfort. "I don't know why, but it never occurred to me that you wouldn't know. The papers in Indiana were filled with it for days, but I guess down here he wouldn't have gotten more than a passing mention on a back page somewhere."

"Why didn't you tell me?" His voice was still harsh with shock.

In spite of herself, Kailin had to laugh. "You didn't exactly give me an opportunity, Brett."

He flushed again. What must it be like for him, Kailin wondered, finding himself face-to-face with her after all these years with no warning at all? She at least had been given some time to prepare herself, but he was still reeling from the shock, lashing out blindly as he struggled to come to terms with having her in his life again.

"I'm sorry." She blinked, realized he was looking down at her, a frown wedged solidly between his brows. "It's just that seeing you again brought it all back, Kailin. That's not an excuse, it's just a fact. For eleven years I haven't been able to get the image out of my mind of the two of you together, and when I saw you this morning..." He shook his head wearily and stared off into the distance. "Hell, I don't know. It's been eating me up inside, I guess. Knowing he had you and I didn't."

"You were always there between us," she whispered, not having the faintest clue why she was telling him this. It was none of his business, especially after what he'd said this morning, but for some reason it seemed right that he know. "Royce was terrified you'd come riding out of the mists one day and spirit me away. I don't think he ever really believed I'd married him instead of you."

"He wasn't the only one." His voice was rough. He turned to look at her, eyes unreadable.

Kailin's gaze faltered. A light breeze fingered her hair, scented by rain and the sea. "I didn't think you cared," she said softly.

"Damn it, Kailin—" He stopped, as though he'd caught himself about to say something he didn't want to.

"You never came after me," she whispered, rubbing her fingers along the railing.

"Oh, I came, all right." His voice was just a breath of sound right behind her. "Kailin, I was after you like a hound on a fox, with your old man running interference all the way. But I was too late. When I finally figured out what was going on, you were Mrs. Royce McGuire.''

"My father told me you'd left, that I'd turned into more trouble than you were interested in handling.''

"You sure as hell were that," he growled. "And you believed him?''

"I didn't know what to believe by then." She looked up at the cloud-quilted sky, feeling suddenly very tired.

"Mo-om!" There was a rush of footsteps, and Becky raced up the steps like a miniature hurricane, all arms and legs and flying golden hair.

Kailin looked around and was just about to say something to her daughter when she caught sight of Brett's face. And froze. He had wheeled around and was staring at the girl as though a bomb had gone off, his expression holding such indescribable expectancy that Kailin's heart literally stopped beating.

Four

⎯⎯⎯⎯

Everything was happening all wrong! Kailin whispered in her mind. She'd hoped to warn him about Becky before they met, but now it was too late.

The girl reached the top of the stairs in a burst of energy, radiating exuberance as a stove radiates heat. "Hey, Mom, can we—whoops!" She saw Brett and stopped dead. Then, unabashed, she grinned even wider. "Sorry."

"Becky," Kailin said quietly. "This is—"

"Brett Douglass." Becky's eyes shone. "Oh, wow, this is too much! You look exactly like your pictures. And you look a lot better without that dumb beard."

"This," Kailin said with a dry smile, "is my ever-tactful daughter, Rebecca. She's staying down here with me for a few days over Thanksgiving, then will head back up to Indiana to stay with her grandparents when school starts again."

Becky made a face, then grinned at Brett. "Everyone calls me Becky. Did you really chain yourself to the gates of

Grandad Yarbro's plant? Mom says you even went to jail once. She says—''

''Becky, for heaven's sake!'' Kailin protested.

''Sorry,'' Becky said, not looking sorry in the least. ''But it's so great actually seeing you. I mean, I've heard so much about you and—'' She stopped at a look from Kailin, grinning unrepentantly.

''She can be a little overwhelming at times,'' Kailin said with a laugh. ''But after Royce died I used to dig out all my old picture albums, and I'd tell her about all the crazy things we used to do.'' Brett gave her such an odd look that she blushed self-consciously. ''I guess you—your memory— helped me through some hard times. And you know how kids are fascinated by the things their parents did when *they* were young. Becky could never get enough of it—'' Kailin stopped.

Brett's memory *had* helped get her through the nightmare months after Royce had been killed, but that hadn't been the only reason she'd spent long hours going through those albums, reading the letters, daydreaming of what had been—of what might have been. And it wasn't the only reason she regretted having said anything about it now. Showing that hint of her own vulnerability was bad enough, but what was worse—infinitely worse—was that Brett very obviously thought she'd told Becky about him because he was her father....

Entranced, he was staring at the girl in front of him, his expression so filled with wonder that it made Kailin's heart ache. Becky was tall for her age, seemingly consisting of nothing but long, tanned limbs and masses of silver-gold hair exactly the same color as her own. It would be easy to believe she was a year older than her nine years.

She had to tell him the truth. But how? When?

''Kailin! Glad I caught you!''

Kailin turned toward the voice in relief, grateful for the interruption. Linda McAllister was standing just below them, shading her eyes with her hand as she grinned up at Kailin. Her freckled nine-year-old daughter was beside her, and Kailin smiled at them both. "Hi, you two!"

"How about coming to a movie with us tonight?" Linda called up.

"I'd love to, but I'm up to my ears in work!"

"Can Becky come?" Peggy McAllister piped up hopefully.

"That's a great idea," Linda said. "She can stay over tonight, and tomorrow morning I'll take them both over to the craft and art fair down at the community center."

Becky's eyes widened. "Oh, can I, Mom?"

Kailin laughed. "I don't know why not. You're sure it won't be any trouble, Linda?"

"Hardly!" Linda assured her. "It's great having someone Peggy's age around."

"Come on, Becky," Peggy cried, everything settled to her satisfaction. "There's this real neat parrot over by the restaurant that talks and everything!"

Becky started toward the stairs, then paused and gave Kailin a sly sidelong look. "With me out of the way, you can invite Brett over."

"Rebecca..." Kailin said, her voice rising warningly.

Becky grinned. "See you tomorrow! And it was nice finally meeting you, Dr. Douglass."

Brett swept off an imaginary hat and bowed deeply, clicking his heels. "Until we meet again, fair maiden."

Becky giggled with delight, then galloped down the stairs, pausing at the bottom to wave.

"Thanks, Linda," Kailin called after the three of them. "I'll call you tomorrow."

"It hasn't taken you long to make friends."

Kailin smiled and turned to look at Brett. "Sheer luck, actually. Linda's husband owns a manufacturing plant in Virginia. I did some troubleshooting there a couple of years ago and Linda and I got to be friends. It's just coincidence that they're down here for a couple of weeks while Becky and I are here, but it's great for the kids.''

Brett was still staring after Becky, his expression wistful. ''She's beautiful.''

''Yes, she is.'' Kailin hesitated, biting her lower lip as she realized she didn't have an inkling of what to say next. All her worst nightmares about seeing Brett again hadn't prepared her for *this*. It had never occurred to her that he would think Becky was his; after all, he hadn't even believed she was pregnant!

But she'd been wrong about that, too. Kailin took a deep breath, bracing herself. He'd not only finally believed her, he'd gone looking for her—only to find her married to Royce. Oh, Brett, she whispered silently, how you must have hated me. And all those years I hated you, thinking you didn't care. ''Brett, there's something I have to—''

''Taking the afternoon off, Douglass?'' Kailin glanced around as Craig Bryant strolled toward them. He grinned at her, oblivious to her unwelcoming scowl, and slipped his arm around her waist. ''You never gave me an answer about supper tonight, Kailin.''

Catching sight of the expression on Brett's face, Kailin groaned inwardly. Great timing, Craig, she thought savagely. Her annoyance was intensified by the knowledge that Craig had done it on purpose, and that Brett, the big oaf, had fallen for it hook, line and proverbial sinker.

She eased herself from Craig's embrace and picked up her briefcase. ''Something's come up, Craig, I'm sorry.''

Craig's face darkened. ''Something or someone?''

Brett's face was like granite. ''Ease off, Bryant. You're walking on thin ice.''

''Staking a claim, Douglass?'' Craig's eyebrow arched. ''In case you hadn't noticed, I was here first.''

''In case neither of you Neanderthals had noticed,'' Kailin cut in impatiently, ''this is the Twentieth Century. If anyone's claim gets staked, I'll be the one doing the staking."

"Look, Kailin, what's going on here?" Craig glared at her belligerently. "You and Douglass got something going I don't know about?"

"Bryant..." Brett took a catlike step toward the other man.

"You stay the hell out of this, Douglass. I'm sick and tired of you dogging my tracks everywhere I go!"

Kailin didn't even see what started it. One moment Craig and Brett were standing nose-to-nose like two rutting stags, and in the next Craig's fist caught Brett squarely on the side of his jaw. He staggered back with a grunt of pain, then regained his balance, drew his right arm back and threw a punch at Craig's outthrust chin that had every ounce of his 170-odd pounds behind it.

"Brett!" Kailin gasped as Craig landed flat on his back. He lay there staring at the overhanging roof, unmoving. "My God, you've killed him!"

"Killed him, hell!" snarled Brett, shaking his right fist furiously. "I should break his damned neck!"

"Not on my property," came a low growl from behind them. Zac Cheevers strode toward them, teeth clamped down on the ever-present cigar. "Damn it, boy, if you're going to kill a man, don't do it in front of your lawyer's office. Take him out into the swamp somewhere and stuff him under a mangrove root."

Craig sat up slowly, groaning. "I think he broke my nose." He touched it gingerly, then examined his fingers for blood.

"I didn't come anywhere near your nose," Brett growled through gritted teeth. He was still cradling his fist painfully. "But I'd be happy to oblige."

"That's enough." Zac caught Brett's arm and pulled him back roughly. "If you two young bucks want to have it out, fine—it's long overdue. But take it somewhere else. And

leave *her*—'' he thrust his bull-like head toward Kailin
''—out of it. Fighting over a principle is one thing, fighting
over a woman is purely stupid.'' He pulled Craig to his feet.
''Now you get the hell off my property.''

Craig left, giving Brett a ferocious glare that earned him
a muttered curse. ''Damn young fools,'' Zac muttered. He
looked at Kailin. ''This is the kind of trouble we don't need
right now. I suppose you realize that.'' Then he gave a snort
of laughter and turned away, shaking his big gray head in
amusement. ''Can't blame you, boy,'' he said to Brett as he
walked by him. ''If I was about thirty years younger, you'd
be fightin' me off, too.''

After Zac had disappeared, Kailin took a deep breath and
looked at Brett. ''That,'' she said with precision, ''was just
about the stupidest thing I've ever seen you do.''

Brett looked at his hand, wincing. Then he shook his head
slowly and prodded his jaw. ''I can't believe I did it myself,'' he muttered sheepishly. ''I haven't pulled a stunt like
that in years.''

''About eleven of them, I suspect.'' She took his hand in
hers and examined the swollen, bruised knuckles. ''It's a
miracle you didn't break something.''

He flexed his fingers experimentally. Then his eyes caught
hers and he started to chuckle. The chuckle grew to a deep,
lazy laugh, and Kailin, unable to help herself, joined him.
The stiffness between them melted, and for a moment they
were best friends and lovers again. It had always been like
this between them. It had driven their friends crazy when
their eyes would catch and they'd burst into laughter for no
apparent reason, linked in some special way that tran-
scended spoken words.

Smiling, Kailin put her fingers under his chin and tipped
it up, eyeing the bruise that was already starting to discolor
his jaw. ''Classic Brett Douglass. I'd have thought you'd
learned to duck by now.''

''It's been a long time since I had to.''

"Paradise Point's important to you, isn't it?"

"It's important. But this didn't have anything to do with Paradise Point."

"I know." She touched his bruised hand. "I'd have never accepted Craig's dinner invitation."

"It wouldn't be any of my business if you did."

"I know that, too."

The silence grew taut as wire between them. Kailin could feel his warm breath stir her hair, could smell the leathery cologne he was wearing. It seemed to fold around her, drawing her into him, and without even thinking about what she was doing she lowered her head and kissed his swollen knuckles. She rested her lips on each in turn, then delicately ran the tip of her tongue along them.

She heard him swallow. He cupped her head with his other hand and slowly drew her against him until her forehead rested on his chest. She felt dizzy and had to fight for every breath, aware of nothing but the pressure of his hand, the touch of his mouth against her hair. The deep, regular thud of his heart seemed to vibrate through every atom in her body, and she slowly relaxed against him, not daring to do more than breathe.

Kailin had no idea how long they stood like that, caught in an otherworldly reality that excluded everything but the two of them. She thought she heard him whisper her name and tried to answer, but the breath caught in her throat as his fingers tangled in her hair and he pressed her tightly to him.

Then, slowly, the real world intruded, a bit at a time: the bark of a dog, a woman's laughter, the startled cry of a baby. Kailin opened her eyes, aware of the roughness of Brett's denim shirt against her cheek. The pressure of his fingers in her hair eased and she felt him take a deep, uneven breath, as though waking from sleep.

She stepped away from him unsteadily. "I...uh...should get going," she whispered, not looking at him.

"Yeah." He sounded as shaken as she felt. "I've got an irate tomcat back at the clinic awaiting the unkindest cut of all."

"Ouch." Kailin laughed, daring to glance up at him. "Doomed to a life of amorous memories."

"And maybe a few regrets, if he's like the rest of us," Brett said very quietly. He reached out and tipped her chin up with his finger, gazing down at her with a frown. Then, without saying another word, he turned and walked away.

"Glad I talked you into coming?" Jill Benedict Kincaide took a large bite out of the end of Brett's hot dog, then handed it back to him with a smile. "I love country fairs. Food always tastes better outside, doesn't it?"

"I haven't had the chance to find out yet," Brett said, surveying the damage to his frankfurter. "I thought you weren't hungry."

"I'm not." Jill took a long swallow from his soft drink, smiling around the straw. "Not now, anyway. Thanks."

"Kincaide not feeding you properly?" Brett sank his teeth into what was left of his meal with enthusiasm.

Jill laughed. "He's feeding me just fine. You still mad because I ran off and married him instead of you?"

"I've thought of eliminating him a couple of times," Brett assured her conversationally. "I'm always in the market for a good-looking woman who knows her way around a lab. Besides, we could use an extra hand tagging water birds over in the conservation area."

"You're always in the market for a good-looking woman, period," Jill teased. "And I had my fill of wading around mangrove swamps counting alligator eggs and banding egrets while I was down here a year ago. I'm quite happy puttering around my research lab and being a wife and mother."

"It shows." Brett slipped his arm around her shoulders. "I'm glad you two worked it out, Jill. I like happy endings."

"With thanks to you." She smiled up at him. "If you'd been less honorable, Brett Douglass, you'd have kept me all to yourself and Hunt and I would never have gotten back together."

"Except he'd always have had your heart. I'd have been second best, and second best in love isn't love at all." He tightened his arm around Jill as he found himself thinking of Kailin. *Was* it possible that she'd really loved him eleven years ago? That she'd married Royce McGuire because she'd felt betrayed and abandoned at a time when she'd needed someone the most? And what was she doing down here now? Was it simple coincidence that had brought her back into his life again, or was there something else going on, something to do with Paradise Point?

Damn it, this was driving him crazy! He'd lain awake half the night trying to unravel all the possibilities and was no closer to an answer this morning. Half of him wanted to believe her, and half of him mistrusted everything she said. He sighed and rubbed his forehead wearily.

"You're brooding." Jill slid her arm around his waist and hugged him. "What's an old bachelor like you doing pondering the intricacies of love, anyway? Something going on in your life I should know about?"

"No. And yes, I *am* glad you talked me into coming down here." His gesture took in the loud, enthusiastic mob surrounding them.

Dozens of colorful booths and exhibit tables had been set up around the small community center, and the overflow had poured into the huge vacant lot across Periwinkle Way. There seemed to be hundreds of people there, all laughing and chattering as they strolled from one craft exhibit to the next or wandered arm in arm, simply enjoying the sunshine. The air was redolent with the tang of mustard and relish and the sweet scent of spun sugar candy. Brett discovered to his surprise that he *was* enjoying himself.

A puff of warm wind curled around them, scented with pine pitch and the sea, and he smiled. "I needed this."

"I know. You've been in another world for days, Brett. I'm worried about you."

"Everything's great," he lied, knowing by Jill's expression that she wasn't taken in. Letting his smile fade, he sighed and gave her shoulder a squeeze as they strolled through the crowd. "I'll survive. She'll be leaving soon and I'll be back to normal."

"She?" Jill stopped dead. "I knew it! I *told* Hunt you were showing all the classic symptoms of woman trouble. What's going on, Brett? Who is she?"

Cursing himself for not keeping his mouth shut, Brett simply smiled. "Just an old acquaintance." *And some old memories...*

Jill eyed him assessingly. "I'll be damned. You *have* been bitten, haven't you?"

Why deny it? Brett asked himself glumly. Last night he'd finally had to admit to himself that he was still halfway in love with Kailin McGuire. Why and how, God alone knew. He'd thought he'd gotten her out of his system long ago, but it must be like malaria, lying dormant for years before something set it off again. All it had taken was one look into those grass-green eyes yesterday and he'd known he wanted her as badly as he ever had.

Like a moth to a candle, he reminded himself grimly.

Again he shook himself free of it. He looked down at Jill and grinned. "How come with all the miracle cures you hotshot scientists are always coming up with you've never found a vaccine against broken hearts?"

Jill gave a snort of laughter. "That bad, huh?"

"That bad."

"Anything I can do?"

"Besides cutting my throat and putting me out of my misery?"

"She married?"

"Not anymore."

"In love with someone else?"

Brett thought of Craig Bryant. "Not that I know of."

"Then I don't see what the problem is."

"It just isn't that easy," he said quietly.

"Does she love you?"

"Jill—" He caught her expression and swallowed the protest. "In her own way, maybe she did once. But now?" He shrugged. "Who knows? Like I said, it isn't that easy."

"Once?" Jill's eyes narrowed. "Just how long have you been suffering this affliction, anyway?"

"About eleven years."

"Eleven *years*?" Jill stopped so suddenly that Brett nearly ran into her. "God, Brett! You've been in love with this woman for eleven years and still don't know how she feels?"

"I never said I loved her," Brett muttered.

"Don't be ridiculous." Jill slipped her arm through his and started walking again. "It's written all over you. And a man doesn't stay in love with a woman for eleven years unless it's the real thing."

The real thing? Brett smiled inwardly. Jill was a classic scientist, able to distill anything down to its most basic components. But there were still some things that defied analysis. Love was one of them. Kailin McGuire was another.

"You stealing my wife, Douglass?"

Brett glanced up to find Hunter Kincaide lounging against a nearby hamburger concession stand, his grin lazy and warm. He was cradling a sleeping baby against one shoulder and a large stuffed rabbit against the other, carrying off the apparent contradiction between the hard-boiled investigative reporter and the doting father with élan.

"I've been trying my damnedest," Brett assured him with a slashing grin, "but she won't have me."

Jill laughed and slipped the baby out of Hunt's grasp. "Our fearless bachelor veterinarian here is in love."

"Jill, I am *not* in—"

Hunter gave a snort of laughter and clapped Brett solidly on the shoulder. "Just ignore it, Douglass. It's called post-natal euphoria, and the symptoms include seeing everything through a rosy haze, being convinced the entire world is in love and trying to marry off all your single friends. Everyone in Washington runs when they see her coming."

"Liar." Jill gave Hunter a poke in the ribs with her elbow, then slipped Brett a teasing look. "I expect a wedding invitation within six months, or I'm coming back down here to raise hell, got that?"

"Yes, ma'am," Brett retorted smartly. "Do you bully Kincaide like this?"

"All the time," Hunter said fondly, giving his wife a hug.

Watching the two of them sharing teasing smiles, cradling their child between them, Brett felt a pang of sadness shoot through him. When he'd first met Jill she'd been numb with hurt, her career shattered. For nearly seven months she'd wandered around like a victim of shell shock, trying to put the pieces of her life together, torn between love and hate for the tall, gray-eyed man now standing beside her. But Hunter Kincaide, thank God, had refused to let her go. He'd followed her to Sanibel with the tenacity that had earned him the nickname of Bulldog Kincaide, and he'd hung on until they'd faced the problems and misunderstandings that had torn them apart.

He watched Kincaide smile down at his sleeping son, Jill tucked comfortably into the curve of his arm, and felt another stabbing ache run through him—of regret this time. All those wasted years, he found himself thinking. All those years when Royce McGuire had been raising Becky, seeing her first smile, her first step, listening to her first tentative words.

Damn.

He had to catch his breath at the sense of utter loss that arrowed through him. And Becky? Where did she fit into his life now, or he into hers?

He shook his head. He could go on trying to rework the past for the next twenty years, but the bottom line was what was best for Becky. He'd walked out on Kailin eleven years ago. He hadn't even believed her when she'd told him she was pregnant. Kailin had done the best she could. He had no right. No right at all. And yet . . . watching Jill and Hunter, he had the sudden, impulsive urge to find Kailin, to talk with her, to plan—

"Are you all right?" Brett blinked, realized Jill was peering up at him worriedly. "Hunt and I are going sailing this afternoon. Interested in coming with us? You look like you could use an afternoon with friends. To talk, maybe..."

Brett ruffled her tousled hair with his hand, grinning. "Thanks, but I've got things to do. There's someone here this afternoon I have to talk to."

Jill's face lighted up, and she gave a soft, knowing laugh. "Six months at the latest, Douglass. I mean it." Then, before Brett could say anything, she slipped her arm through Hunter's and tugged him into the crowd, sparing Brett a sly wink before she disappeared.

Brett found himself laughing at Jill's indefatigable belief in the marvels of love. But how do you recognize it when you find it? he felt like shouting after her. How do you separate reality from wishful thinking, truth from lie? And how do you ever learn to trust again?

"It's a Spanish piece of eight," the jeweler said. "Salvaged off a galleon that went down off the Keys in 1675. We have certificates of authenticity and provide you with a numbered photo of the piece to identify it for insurance purposes.''

Kailin turned the old coin in her fingers. It was worn and irregular, but she could still make out the markings on it. It had been mounted in a narrow border of gold. The jeweler slipped a gold chain through the loop, and Kailin held it up to her throat to admire it in a hand mirror. ''It's beautiful!''

''If you want an outside opinion, take it.'' Two tanned hands slipped around her throat and took the chain from her fingers, startling Kailin so badly that she nearly dropped the mirror.

''Brett!''

''Gorgeous.'' He took his hands away from the clasp and let them rest lightly on the bare skin of her shoulders, his eyes holding hers in the mirror. ''And so's the pendant.''

The touch of his hands was like fire. It seemed impossible that such an innocent gesture could rattle her, but Kailin found herself tongue-tied and breathless. Feeling herself blush, she tipped the mirror hastily so that it reflected only the coin. It glowed like fire on her sun-burnished skin, and she found herself nodding.

''You're right.'' To her relief, her voice sounded almost normal. ''I'll take it.''

To her simultaneous relief and regret, Brett drew his hands from her. Her skin tingled as though she'd gotten too much sun, although she knew that wasn't the reason. You're acting like an idiot, she advised herself calmly. At thirty you're supposed to be immune to all this silliness, not melting into a puddle at the mere touch of a man's hand. Not even *this* man's hands.

Brett stepped around her and leaned one elbow on the display case, looking at the pendant, which was still around her throat. Kailin picked up the mirror and looked at it again, trying to ignore the way his eyes were moving leisurely from the pendant to the bare sweep of her shoulders above the ruffled bodice of her sundress. "No lecture on how I'm contributing to the destruction of offshore archaeological sites?"

"I've mellowed." His teeth flashed in a teasing grin. "Besides, that coin is displayed much more effectively around your throat than in some dusty museum."

"You *have* mellowed." She lifted an eyebrow as she removed the pendant and handed it to the jeweler. "In the past you'd have been picketing this place."

"Then I thought you could fight the battle on all fronts at once and still win. I've learned to focus my firepower on one or two major skirmishes at a time."

"Like Paradise Point?"

"Like Craig Bryant. There's a difference."

Kailin looked at him seriously. "I'm glad you realize that."

"You know this guy?" the jeweler asked Kailin, nodding at Brett.

Brett grinned, his eyes capturing Kailin's. "Oh, yes, she knows me."

There was no mistaking the intimacies that simple statement encompassed, and to Kailin's intense annoyance she felt herself color again.

"Well, in that case..." The jeweler did some rapid calculations, then quoted her a price that was substantially lower than the original one. He grinned sheepishly. "I charge the tourists a little more."

"No kidding! Knowing Brett Douglass takes me out of that unenviable classification, does it?"

"Knowing Brett Douglass makes you practically family," the jeweler assured her with a laugh. "He saved my old dog a couple of years ago after he tangled with a gator." He cupped the pendant in his palm. "Would you like it in a box?"

A few minutes later, pendant tucked in her handbag, Kailin looked up at Brett and smiled. "Thank you. If I'd known being an acquaintance of yours was the key to getting great bargains, I'd have been name-dropping all morning."

Brett's laugh was throaty. "There's still all afternoon, if you'd like some company." He paused, then added very casually, "Unless you're already with someone."

Kailin gave him a tolerant look. "You never used to be this tactful, Douglass. To answer the question you didn't ask, no, I am not here with Craig Bryant."

Brett gazed down at her calmly. "The man's a hustler and a punk, Kailin. Don't fall for his smooth line."

"I wasn't intending to," she assured him dryly. "I'm a good deal older than when you knew me last, Brett. I don't fall for anyone's smooth line anymore."

He gave her a lazy, appraising glance. "That meant for me?"

"It was a general observation."

He nodded and shoved his hands into the back pockets of his jeans, strolling along beside her as relaxed as a cat. It didn't take Kailin long to realize that Brett knew most of the people there. The mob parted before them as the Red Sea had before Moses, and almost everyone had a word to say, a smile, a nod of the head. Everyone from gray-haired matrons to toddlers knew him by name, and he returned the greetings with the relaxed congeniality of a man comfortable in the community.

"Is there anyone here you don't know?" she asked, a trifle testy, as a gorgeous redhead in the tiniest shorts and the skimpiest French-cut T-shirt imaginable drifted across their path.

Brett wrestled his gaze from the redhead's decorative retreat and blinked, looking down at her. "What did you say? Sorry."

"If I'm in the way, Douglass, just say the word."

He grinned lazily and dropped his arm around her shoulders, tugging her gently against him. "I wouldn't detect the merest trace of jealousy, would I?"

"Of course not," she retorted airily. "Why on earth would I be jealous?" *Why indeed*, an inner voice asked with almost gleeful spite. She ignored it and gave him a speculative glance. "You *do* have a certain, reputation...."

"You probably won't believe this, but I haven't had a relationship with a woman—a *serious* relationship—in over two years."

"And what about the nonserious ones?" she asked flippantly.

"Dinner, a drink or two, maybe some dancing. Then home. Alone." He looked down at her, his eyes serious. "Rumor has it I'm living the classic bachelor's life. But the truth is, I spend most of my nights with no one but my old dog for company."

"Most?" Kailin groaned. "I can't believe I just said that! Sorry..."

"I never said I was perfect," Brett said with a teasing laugh. "Once in a long, long while, Kailin. That's all."

"It isn't any of my business."

"No more than your relationship with Bryant was mine."

Why, Kailin asked herself thoughtfully, were they doing this? People usually got things like old lovers out of the way if they were planning on starting something, not simply as afternoon chitchat. "How come you're still on the loose, anyway? I'd have thought some beach goddess would have snapped you up years ago."

"Maybe I'm still in love with you, Kailin."

He said it easily, his grin flashing in the sunlight, and Kailin laughed. "Are you flirting with me, Douglass?"

"Hard to break old habits." His eyes caught hers, aglow with old memories. "Especially enjoyable ones."

The words had a rough, smokey edge to them, and she remembered with sudden clarity the way he'd growled her name while they'd been making love, the husky catch to his voice when he'd whispered those deliciously explicit things....

"Do you—do you think we could get something to eat?" she asked unsteadily, hoping he didn't have any idea of what she'd just been thinking. Damn it, what was the matter with her! It was difficult enough trying to appear calm and in control without having her mind dart off onto these erotic little side trips. She slipped Brett a curious glance, wondering if he was having the same problem. Maybe that was why his mood kept shifting, silently hostile one moment, antagonistic the next, then this gentle, almost wistful teasing. It was like sharing a cage with a tiger and never knowing what to expect. It was keeping her so off balance that she felt dizzy.

"Does a hot dog sound all right?" Brett asked lightly.

"A hot dog sounds fantastic! With relish, mustard and lots of onions?"

"Is there any other way?"

"Not in any civilized universe." She slipped her arm through his. "You always did know the way to my heart."

"I knew two or three ways," Brett murmured with a chuckle. "Although I don't remember mustard and onions being involved." His eyes met hers. "Chocolate sauce, yes. But mustard and onions...?"

"Brett!" Kailin sputtered with laughter, her cheeks burning as the memories of that night came flooding back. "I think I'd like just a hot dog, all right?"

"For now."

Kailin threw him a sharp, puzzled glance, and Brett had to smile. Just what the hell he thought he was doing, he didn't know. Flirting with her was one thing, but he was sailing very close to dangerous waters with all these sly little inuendos and reminiscences. It was as though he were deliberately taunting himself, seeing how near he could get to the past before the pain started.

Smiling, he recalled when he'd been a kid and every winter there had been a dare made as to who could bring his tongue nearest the frosted wrought-iron fence around the schoolyard without actually touching it. And every winter they had all miscalculated and wound up glued to the thing. It had been an act of courage, and he could still remember the thrill of excitement that had preceded the agony of getting free. He looked down at Kailin. Was that what he was doing now, testing himself? Seeing how close he could get without being burned?

If so, he was living proof that boys could grow into men without learning a hell of a lot along the way.

Kailin was frowning and he said, "I don't remember you getting this uptight when I flirted with you before, sweetheart."

"You just keep me off balance, that's all," she said quietly. "Yesterday you made it plain that even doing business with me was a major irritation, and today..." She shrugged.

"Yesterday I was too surprised at seeing you again to feel much of anything. But today..." He mimicked her shrug. "You're an attractive woman, Kailin McGuire. It's a beautiful day, in spite of the fact we're going to get a hell of a rainstorm before the afternoon's out, and I don't have any pressing emergency that needs my attention." She nodded, still not looking entirely convinced that his good mood was going to last, and he smiled. "Do I recall a request for a hot dog? Mustard. Relish. Lots of onions." She nodded again and he draped his arm comfortably around her shoulder, enjoying the feel of her tucked close against him. Just like old times.

Relax and enjoy it, he told himself as they made their way through the crowd toward a hot dog stand. Common sense said he was asking for trouble, but for the time being, who cared?

Five

Kailin was still quiet when she took the hot dog from his hand a few minutes later. He bought a couple of soft drinks then eased her out of the crowd and into the relative quiet beneath the tall Australian pines bordering the grassy field that made up the temporary parking lot.

It was about ten degrees cooler in the shade and a salty breeze whispered through the lacy foliage. Brett turned his face to it gratefully, sipping the soft drink. Leaning against the trunk of the nearest tree, he rested his booted foot on the wide bumper of a pickup truck parked beside them and smiled down at Kailin. "Better?"

She nodded enthusiastically, her mouth full, and Brett laughed and reached down to wipe a smear of mustard from her chin. "I was starved!" she said a moment later, licking at the mustard and relish trickling between her fingers. "Want a bite?"

Watching her, Brett shook his head. The muscles in his stomach pulled tight as she drew the tip of her tongue along leaving and ... well, who knows? Go tearing after you, perhaps. He wanted me safely and respectably married, and he moved so fast I was Mrs. Royce McGuire before the ink was even dry on the contract he and my new father-in-law had signed.''

"Contract?'' Brett felt something cold spill through his guts. ''What kind of ... contract?''

Kailin smiled wearily. ''I was never anything more to my father than a commodity, like a string of glass beads: something to be bartered when the price was right. An unmarried daughter is only as valuable as her worth and he could see mine going steadily downhill as the summer progressed.'' She glanced up at him. ''I was also on the verge of becoming a family embarrassment.''

Then she looked away, toying with the bottle. ''Sterling McGuire had his problems, too—a youngest son who couldn't do anything right. McGuire needed some out-of-the-way job where Royce couldn't do much damage but which was still respectable enough not to embarrass the family.'' She paused, as though choosing her words carefully. ''So they made a deal. McGuire would provide a socially acceptable husband for Yarbro's knocked-up and rebellious young daughter, and Yarbro would in return provide a job for McGuire's inept son. All very tidy, and all very hush-hush.'' She smiled bitterly. ''My father never did believe in that old adage about marriages being made in heaven.''

Brett's oath was magnificently and creatively obscene.

''He was terrified I'd do something crazy—like running off with you.'' She laughed. ''I couldn't have come up with a more effective statement against him than to run off with his archenemy, the infamous angry young man himself. But I should have known he'd figure out a way to plug up the escape before I actually did it.'' Her smile faded, and she looked down. ''He ... he found out about the baby a couple of weeks before I told you. Our family doctor had been

his golf partner for twenty years, and a little thing like patient confidentiality doesn't count when your friend's
daughter has gotten herself pregnant by a long-haired rebel
from the wrong side of town."

Brett swore again, this time in weary resignation. "That's
why he came to me that night. He knew if he got to me first
and convinced me you weren't pregnant that I'd fall for it.
He *knew* how I'd react—just like he knew every move you'd
make." He gave a snort of harsh laughter, filled with an
empty, hopeless rage. "I wonder if he really thought I'd take
that ten grand he offered me. It didn't matter, really, as long
as *you* believed I'd taken it. He led us through that whole
thing step-by-step."

"If I'd only told you earlier! If I'd gone to you as soon as
I found out, maybe..."

"Who knows? We had as much chance against an old
warrior like your father as a rabbit against a wolf." He
glanced up at her, smiling faintly. "Just out of curiosity,
why *didn't* you tell me right away?"

"I was afraid to," she said simply. "There was no excuse
for my getting pregnant except carelessness. You usually
took care of things, but a couple of times when we just got
carried away, I told you it was safe even though it wasn't
really. I knew better, but..." She smiled suddenly, a faint
blush caressing her cheeks. "It's hard to be very logical at
times like that."

Brett had to laugh, and Kailin's blush deepened. "I finally started taking birth control pills, but by then it was too
late. I wanted the baby, but I didn't know if I should tell you
or... just stop seeing you."

"But why, Kailin?" Brett asked hoarsely. "Damn it, I
loved you! You say you loved me. Why—?"

"I was afraid you'd think I was trying to pressure you into
a commitment you weren't ready to make," she said quietly. "You used to tell me all your plans and dreams, Brett,
all the things you wanted to accomplish—but they never in-

cluded me. You never mentioned love or marriage or the future."

Brett hung his head, shaking it slowly. "When I think of the things I said to you that night..."

"It was like all my nightmares come true," she whispered. "All the way over to your apartment I kept telling myself I was silly to be so nervous. That everything was going to be perfect. Then...you just looked at me with the coldest expression I've ever seen. When you didn't believe me, I felt like my world had been ripped apart."

"Oh, Kailin." He ached with a bone-deep cold, trying to comprehend what she must have felt that night, knowing he'd never be able even to come close. *Kailin, Kailin...what have I done to you?*

"When I got home, Dad took one look at me and knew exactly what had happened. Looking back, it's no surprise, considering he'd planned it all. But at the time he seemed very wise and very sympathetic, and I was in such shock it never occurred to me to wonder why. Common sense says he should have been after you with the 12-gauge and a brace of hounds." Her smile faded almost as quickly as it had blossomed. "Anyway, he told me how lucky I was, that you'd just been using me as a weapon against him, that if I thought you'd ever marry me I was a romantic fool...and so on and so on. He told me you were just a user and that you'd never settle down."

"And six days later you were married."

She just nodded, her head tucked down so that he couldn't see her face. "I started crying halfway through the ceremony and didn't stop for two solid days. Poor Royce must have been ready to kill both my father and me, but he just brought me gallons of hot tea and told me I'd get over you eventually. Then I woke up one morning and realized I wasn't Kailin Yarbro anymore and that I better get on with being my husband's wife."

Kailin looked at him with pain-filled eyes. "I thought you'd taken the money Dad had offered you and had just left town...."

"I worshiped the damned ground you walked on, Kailin." Brett didn't even realize he was going to kiss her until he felt her lips under his. He'd reached out to cup her cheek in his palm, and before he knew what he was doing he'd slipped his hand behind her head and pulled her gently toward him. There was a moment's resistance, then a soft inward sigh of pleasure, and her mouth was there, lips already parting.

She was as sweet as he'd remembered, the moist tip of her tongue reaching hesitantly toward his, touching. He circled it with his and she gave a tiny shudder and melted against him, the slow, liquid thrust of her tongue against his so vibrantly and explicitly sensual that it nearly pushed him over the edge then and there.

He groaned, half in wonder and half in very real agony as his body responded strongly to the so-familiar taste of her. His fingers flexed in her hair, lifting her toward him, and he felt her shiver, tasted the sudden coppery bite of her desire as she kissed him back with the same sudden, unrestrained need.

She whispered something against his mouth, but he didn't hear what it was, didn't care what it was, didn't care about anything but feeling her against him. All his best intentions about resisting dissolved, and in that instant there was absolutely no reality at all but having her in his arms again.

It was Kailin who heard the giggles first. She wrenched her mouth from Brett's and gasped an inarticulate warning, so light-headed she couldn't even remember for a moment where they were. Brett's eyes were inches from hers, the heat in them fading under a faintly puzzled expression. She smiled. "I think," she murmured, "that we've been discovered."

Brett pulled back so suddenly that he sent one of the soft drink bottles flying, and the two girls watching them burst into a deluge of fresh giggles. "Hi, Mom." Becky's grin threatened to take wing.

"Hello, Becky," Kailin said with as much dignity as possible. She smiled at the small, freckled girl standing beside Becky. "How are you, Peggy?"

"Just fine, Mrs. McGuire." Peggy gazed up at Brett. "Hi, Dr. Douglass. Are you enjoying the fair?"

"Very much," Brett assured her dryly. "You two girls having fun?"

"Not as much as *some* people," Becky put in with dancing eyes. "Sorry we ... umm ... interrupted."

"Ready to go home?" Kailin asked mildly.

"Actually," Peggy put in, "we wanted to ask if Becky can stay over at my place again tonight. Mom said it would be okay because then the two kittens won't be—" She gave a squeak as Becky buried an elbow in her ribs, then stood gazing innocently at Kailin.

It was then Kailin realized that in spite of the heat Peggy had her cotton jacket zippered to the throat. It was oddly lumpy, and even as Kailin looked at it one of the lumps moved. "What," she asked with growing suspicion, "are you two up to?"

"Nothing," Becky said with wide-eyed innocence. "Except..."

"Except?"

"Well..." The two girls looked at each other. Then Peggy unzipped her jacket and reached gingerly inside. She withdrew her hand and passed something to Becky.

The black-and-white kitten wailed and peered around nearsightedly. Becky whispered reassuringly to it and cradled it against her chest.

"Rebecca..."

"There were only two left," Becky interjected anxiously. "And the lady at the ASPCA booth said if she didn't find homes for them they'd have to be ... well, *you* know!"

"They had some puppies," Peggy explained cheerfully, extricating the other lump from her jacket. This kitten was all black and wailed just as loudly. "And some rabbits."

Becky handed the bit of fur to Kailin. "It's so cute!"

It was that, Kailin had to admit. She cupped the tiny thing in her palms, feeling its heart racing. It peered up at her with its milky blue kitten eyes, its tiny rosebud ears not even fully unbuttoned yet, and mewed softly in distress.

"Its mother got run over," Becky said. "Peggy's mom said she could keep the other one if... well..."

"If I said you could keep this one." Kailin looked at Becky assessingly. "I think your grandfather's been giving you lessons in pressure tactics, Rebecca McGuire."

"Mo-oth-er!"

She made three anxious syllables out of the word, and Kailin cradled the kitten against her cheek to hide her smile. Its fur was like watered silk, and she thought she detected the first rough note or two of a hesitant purr. "Don't wheedle. What's your grandmother going to say if you turn up there after the holidays with a kitten in tow?"

"Grandma likes cats," Becky said pleadingly. "Aw, Mom, please? I'll take good care of it, I promise. I'll feed it and brush it and play with it and—"

"And the litter pan?" The kitten was gnawing industriously on her thumb, clearly over its fright. Its face was all black, except for two white patches on either side of its mouth and two small clumps of white over each eye that gave it a raffish, surprised expression.

"I'll clean it every day," Becky assured her, eyes lighting up with hope. "Please, Mom? Oh, please say yes!"

"Let's have a look." Lifting the kitten out of Kailin's hands, Brett examined it with swift competence. "It's healthy and in good shape. Just needs some love and affection."

"See?" Becky put in swiftly. "And besides, we have a moral obligation. People do so much damage to the planet that when we have a chance to do something good, we should do it."

Kailin looked from Becky to Brett and back again. "Are you two in cahoots?"

"Don't look at me!" Brett protested with a laugh as he handed the kitten back to Kailin. "Your daughter has a well-developed sense of global responsibility, that's all."

"My daughter," Kailin said darkly, "is a con artist."

"Please, Mom?"

Kailin sighed. "If it shreds your grandmother's drapes while you two are up there, you're going to have to take the heat."

"I will!" Becky gave her a fierce hug. "Please? It's a known fact that kids grow up to be well-adjusted adults if they have pets to take care of. You wouldn't want me to grow up to be a bank robber or something, would you?"

"From all the signs, you're going to grow up to be a first-class encyclopedia salesman."

"Sales*lady*," Becky corrected, reaching down to stroke the kitten. "Does that mean I can keep him?"

Weakening, Kailin looked down at the kitten. It gazed back at her sleepily, its tiny paws kneading the ball of her thumb, and broke into a halting, unsteady purr. "Oh, good grief," she muttered in defeat, lifting it up to eye level. "Welcome to the family!"

"Oh, Mom, thanks!" Becky gave Kailin a hug, then gently took the kitten from her. "I'm going to call him Maverick."

"We'll have to buy food and litter and—"

"Oh, that's okay, Mrs. McGuire," Peggy put in happily. "My mom said she'd stop at Bailey's on the way home to pick up all that stuff."

"I have the feeling I've been totally conned," Kailin protested with a laugh. She slipped some money from her wallet and handed it to Becky. "This is for the ASPCA, and this is for whatever Maverick needs."

"And your favorite veterinarian will throw in a free exam, shots and an obligatory lecture on how to care for new kittens," Brett added. "Bring them both around to the office tomorrow."

"Oh, wow, thanks, you guys!" Becky paused long enough to plant a kiss on Kailin's cheek, then she and Peggy danced off. "Come on, Mav. Are you hungry?"

Watching the two girls hurry off, Brett laughed. "Maverick?"

"Tom Cruise's call sign in *Top Gun*," Kailin explained. "At the moment it's her favorite movie."

"She into movie-star crushes already?"

Kailin laughed. "She has a crush on Cruise *and* the plane—she wants to be a naval pilot. A while back she was going to become a marine biologist and study whales, then she decided she wanted to be a bicycle courier. That one lasted a week, I think. For a while she was going to be an astronaut, then an archaelogist. At the moment she's torn between being a fighter pilot and an interpretive dancer—she's studying dance at school and adores her teacher."

Kailin paused. Brett was staring after the two girls, a half smile on his lips, his eyes wistful. She had to tell him, Kailin reminded herself. It wasn't fair letting him think that Becky was his. For eleven years he'd believed that she had gotten rid of his baby as quickly as she'd gotten rid of him, and now he was just as certain she hadn't. It was going to be heart-wrenching having to tell him the truth.

For half a moment she toyed with the idea of never telling him. What harm could come of it? Almost as quickly as the idea occurred to her, she felt ashamed of herself. Not only would she be lying to Brett, she'd be passing that lie on to Becky. It wouldn't be fair either to her or to Royce. All things considered, he'd been a good husband and a good father. He deserved better.

Why, she thought with silent glumness, does life have to be so difficult at times? "Brett," she said quietly, "there's something I have to—"

"It's going to have to wait, sweetheart!" he said with a whoop. "Hang on!" He snatched her hand and pulled her to her feet, then took off across the parking area at a fast lope.

"Brett, for heaven's sake," Kailin sputtered, nearly pulled off her feet. "What are you doing?"

In the next instant, she had her answer. A bolt of lightning ripped the sky and thunder cannonaded around them, making the air shudder. As though jarred loose by the noise, huge drops of icy water started pattering around them.

"My truck's over here somewhere." Brett's fingers tightened around hers. "Run!"

Kailin didn't need the encouragement. Another searing fork of lightning lasered the sky just then, and she flinched as the sky opened and they were deluged by a nearly solid torrent of icy water. Half blinded by the blowing rain and her own hair, she gripped Brett's hand fiercely as they sprinted through the pelting rain toward the blurred outlines of his truck, laughing with exhilaration as they splashed through cold, ankle-deep water.

Brett lifted Kailin into the truck, then clambered in behind her and slammed the door.

"I don't believe this!" Breathless with laughter, Kailin combed her soaking hair back with both hands. Her cotton dress was plastered to her like onionskin, and she plucked at it helplessly.

Brett scrubbed his hands furiously through his hair, spraying water. He rummaged through the clutter behind the seat, then drew out a wool blanket and put it around her shoulders. "You don't mind a few dog hairs, do you?"

Laughing, Kailin wrung a handful of water out of her hair, then started rubbing it with the blanket. "I've heard of monsoons, but this is ridiculous." Gingerly she eased her

feet out of what were once a pair of white canvas espa-
drilles. "Even Noah got some warning."

"It'll let up in a few minutes." Brett's teeth flashed in the
dim light. He pulled his sweatshirt over his head and hung
it across the steering column, where it dripped into the
growing puddle under his feet.

It was raining even harder now. Water sluiced down the
truck windows in solid sheets, curtaining out the world, and
Kailin sighed and tucked one foot under her, relaxing back
against the seat. "All we need is the picnic basket."

Brett chuckled. "You remember that, too, do you?"

"How could I forget?" Kailin slipped him a wry glance.
"It was our first real date. You'd promised me a romantic,
old-fashioned picnic, and you had that huge hamper that
must have cost you an entire week's pay full of cheese and
game hen and champagne. We were going to row across the
lake to the island. I even wore that silly white gauzy dress
because I thought it fit the occasion."

Brett grinned, pulled off his sneakers and dumped the
water out of them. "But when we got to the lake we discovered half the town had the same idea and there were no
rowboats left."

"So we decided to drive up to another lake. Except we
had a flat—"

"And no spare."

"And we got out to walk to the nearest town." Kailin's
grin widened. "I was wearing a pair of unbelievably expensive Italian sandals, four-inch heels and cobweb straps."

"Yeah, sexy as hell." Brett's laugh was deep and rum-
bly. "You got mad after half a mile and threw them in the
ditch, then remembered how much you'd paid for them and
went scrambling after them."

"Caught my dress on a branch and ripped it to shreds.
Then it started to rain." She rested her head on the seat
back, laughing. "It came down as though it hadn't rained

in a month, and there we were on some little dirt side road in the middle of nowhere.''

"But then you saw that old barn and we clambered over a fence to get to it.''

"And found ourselves face-to-face with the biggest bull I've ever seen in my life.''

"And you were so wet and mad you just marched up to him and screamed at him to get out of the way.'' Brett chuckled. "I don't know who you managed to scare more—the bull or me.''

Kailin laughed. "It worked, didn't it?''

"A loft of dry hay never looked so good!''

Kailin turned her head to look at him, smiling. "Everything in the picnic basket was ruined but the grapes and the champagne. I swear I've never eaten a meal since that tasted better.''

Brett reached across and stroked her cheek with his thumb, his eyes warm. "And we made love afterward, for the first time. I've always remembered the sound of the rain on the barn roof and how dry and warm we were, curled up in the hay.''

"I itched for weeks.'' Then, growing serious, she turned her head and kissed his fingers. "That was one of the happiest days of my life. We had magic for a little while that summer, didn't we?''

"Yeah, we had magic.'' He looked down at her for a long, silent while, his fingers still stroking her cheek. "God, I loved you, Kailin,'' he whispered. "There's been nobody since who's even come close to making me feel the way you used to.''

"Oh, Brett.'' She reached up to touch his cheek, feeling herself drawn irresistibly toward those blue, blue eyes. They filled her universe and she could feel his breath on her cheek, her mouth, the featherlike touch of his fingertips as they moved delicately down the curve of her cheek to rest undemandingly on the back of her neck.

Wonderingly, as though tracing the outline of a dream, Kailin ran her fingers along the rugged contours of his face. She touched the spray of fine white lines at the outer corners of his eyes, etched there by sun and wind, the sharp blades of his cheekbones. The upper half was the same face she'd once known by heart; below that it was as new and uncharted as any stranger's. She explored the planes of his cheeks, the long, strong thrust of his jaw. His mouth was the same, still wide and full and as inviting as it had ever been, his lush lower lip dimpled lightly in the center.

He opened his mouth and turned his head very slightly, capturing her finger gently between his lips, his eyes never leaving hers. His mouth was warm and moist, and he touched her fingertip with his tongue, swirled around it, worked against it in a gentle sucking motion that made Kailin go suddenly and unexpectedly weak. She rested her forehead on his arm, which was lying along the back of the truck seat, and made no protest at all when he lifted it and drew her close against him.

Six

___

The skin on his shoulders and chest was slick and cold with rain, yet it was blazing just under the surface. She ran her cheek along his arm until it rested on his shoulder. His hair lay plastered to his neck and around his ears, and she delicately licked away a trickle of rainwater from his neck, feeling him catch his breath.

He murmured her name in a thick, low voice and cupped her head with his other hand, his breathing deepening. Slowly he gathered her soaking hair into a rope at the nape of her neck. Then, even more slowly, he slipped the thin straps of her sundress over her wet shoulders.

Even expecting the moist, warm touch of his mouth, Kailin started slightly. She shivered as he ran a path of lingering kisses from her ear to the point of her shoulder, then slowly back again, his tongue laving the rain water from her skin. He whispered her name against her ear, the very tip of his tongue following its inward curl, and gently tugged her soggy skirt out from beneath her. Slipping his hands under her, he lifted her onto his lap.

There was no mistaking his need, even through the heavy fabric of his jeans, and Kailin had to catch her breath at the intimate touch. She felt the muscles in his inner thighs tighten as she drew her leg up high between his and he whispered something and pressed himself against her. Kailin had to bite her lip to keep from crying out at the unbeliev-ably erotic sensation of the rough denim against her smooth skin.

He knew, she thought dizzily. Even after eleven years, he still knew every move and nuance and touch that could set her afire. Dimly she realized she should be protesting this, but even as she thought it, the words died in her throat. His hands were at the elasticized top of her sundress now, tug-ging it slowly down, and she shivered again in delicious an-ticipation.

"Do you want me to stop?" he murmured.

"N-no."

Brett murmured something again, a coaxing whisper of sound she couldn't make out. She drew back far enough to look up at him questioningly and he smiled, his eyes hooded and smoky, then took her hands and placed them on his bare, muscled stomach. His eyes said the rest, and he caught his breath as she slowly drew the zipper of his jeans down, deliberately running her fingernails lightly down the dark hair on his stomach. Teasing, drawing the anticipation out for him, she folded the flaps of his open jeans back but didn't touch him. Instead she ran her hands back up his stomach to his chest, then his shoulders and neck, to slip her fingers deeply into his thick, wet hair.

She smiled at him, tracing the curve of his lower lip with the tip of her tongue. "Want me to stop?"

"You know the answer to that," he growled roughly. He bent his head and captured that marauding tongue between his lips, drawing it deeply and fiercely into his mouth.

Any last-minute hesitancy that Kailin might have had vanished. It was insane, she told herself as his mouth possessed hers. It couldn't be happening, couldn't be Brett—*her* Brett—locked so intimately against her after all these years. She'd dreamed of it for so long that she was half-afraid to move in case she awoke and discovered it was nothing but a delicious daydream, that the lean, hard body straining against hers was nothing more than a memory.

"Oh, angel, I don't know where you're taking me," Brett breathed. He tugged her dress down, and then her breasts were free, the nipples already hard and sensitive. He cupped them in his hands and she arched her back, her thighs tightening on his. Responding, he shifted around, and Kailin gave a squeak of surprise as she suddenly found herself lying on the truck seat, Brett pressed lithely against her.

"Brett!" She gave another gasp, this time of laughter, as he smoothly pulled her skirt to her hips and drew one of her legs up so that she was cradling him intimately between her thighs. "Brett, you idiot," she whispered, still laughing. "We're too old for this! Teenagers make out in trucks, not sedate types like us!"

"We're never too old for this," he whispered, nuzzling her breasts lovingly.

"But not here, for heaven's sake," she sputtered, laughing.

"Why not?" he growled breathlessly, twisting around so he could kiss her breasts. "We're facing the woods, at the far edge of the lot, and it's pouring rain. Even if anyone was crazy enough to come out here, he couldn't see a thing." He drew his tongue around and under her breast, nipping the taut nipple.

It was true. The windows were curtained by pelting rain and fog and condensation. They were cocooned in a tiny cave of warmth and need, hidden from the world. It was incredibly erotic being half-naked in Brett's arms while life went on about them unsuspecting.

"This is mad!" Laughing, she set her teeth across his earlobe and nipped him gently. "We can't just fall into each other's arms and start making love without...well, without some preliminaries or something."

It was Brett's turn to start laughing. "We're in the middle of preliminaries now, darling. That's what this is...and this." He slipped his large, warm hand under her panties and caressed her bottom, lifting her against him, his touch gently seeking.

Kailin had to catch her breath, clinging to him as his fingers traced a promising filigree on the sensitive skin of her inner thigh. "Brett, I'm serious! How can we just—?"

"Do you feel like we're strangers, Kailin?" He lowered his mouth and brushed his lips across hers again and again. His eyes were glittering slits, and she could feel his heart pounding against her. "If you do, we can stop here and pretend it never happened. If you need time, I'll give you time. If you need wooing, Kailin, I'll woo you. But it's like—"

"Like we've never been apart," she whispered against his mouth. "Oh, Brett, I don't understand any of this, but it's as though the last time we made love was only hours ago."

"I want you, Kailin." The words came out fiercely and sent a melting, honeyed heat through her. "I want to make you mine again. Now. Here. If you want to wait, we will, but—"

"No." She sank her fingers in his hair and pulled his mouth down over hers with the same hot hunger, lifting her hips against him. "No, I don't want to wait. I want you now. I need you now."

Maybe it was the storm, she thought in dazed wonder, or maybe they were simply terrified of losing one another again. But suddenly she knew this was exactly the way it should be, spontaneous and rough and wild. This is the way it had happened the first time, and now they were being given a second chance. It was beyond simple passion and raw need; it was an affirmation of trust, a loving ritual to signify that they were putting the past to rest and committing themselves to starting afresh.

Brett gave a murmur of agreement and slipped his hands under her silky panties, easing them over her bottom. Clammy with rainwater, they resisted his efforts to pull them over her legs until he finally had to sit up and ease them off inch by tantalizing inch.

Kailin sat up, her legs all tangled around his, and slowly ran her palms down his chest and stomach. His eyes narrowed slightly and he swallowed, holding his breath.

"Kailin!" It was almost a cry of pain when she finally, gently touched him. Both fists knotted and he dragged in an unsteady breath as she caressed him sweetly. Then he suddenly grasped her shoulders firmly in both hands. "I'm like a primed powder keg as it is, sweetheart."

Kailin ran her hands around his ribs, up the molded contours of his back. "Brett, this is crazy," she whispered. "We can't make love in here. *No one* can make love in a pickup—it's physically impossible! The cab's too short, the seat's too narrow and—oh!"

With swift, sure competence, he lifted her up and around so that she was lying on her side, then rearranged her legs so she was straddling him, settled himself comfortably against her again. He cradled her in one arm and smiled. "You were saying?" he murmured against her lips, his other hand gliding around the curve of her bottom to press her against him. "Not a lot of room for fancy gymnastics, but plenty of room for the basics." He kissed her, nibbling her lower lip, and slipped his hand further around, his fingers gently seeking. "Like this..."

Kailin sucked her breath in at the first touch, so ready for him that he murmured something in pleasure. "Tell me what you want," he urged. "Tell me how you want it, Kailin. Tell me how much and when." His fingers moved in long, silken caresses that made her feel as though she were spinning off into space, and she moved against him, moaning his name softly. "Don't hold anything back," he whispered. "Go with it as far as it takes you."

There was no intimate, hidden part of her he didn't still know by heart, no special way of loving her he didn't remember. "Make love to me," she murmured against his mouth long minutes later, still trembling with the exquisite magic he'd brought her. "Now, Brett. Make love to me now."

He lay very still for a moment, breathing unsteadily. "Kailin?" he whispered urgently. "Honey, are you ... ?"

She stared at him, not understanding. Then her eyes widened. "Oh, no!" she moaned. "Oh, Brett!"

"No risks this time, sweetheart," he said through gritted teeth. "I lost eleven years ago because we couldn't keep our hands off each other and got careless."

"I don't believe this," she whispered, nearly sobbing.

"Pray." He reached up and around and opened the glove compartment, rummaging through it.

"What?"

"I said pray. I lend my truck to a neighbour's teenage son now and again, and last time I looked in here it was obvious that *he*, at least, *is* prepared for situations like this." He gave a soft groan of relief and curled around to embrace her again, kissing her with a deep and drugging intensity that left no doubt that he'd found what he was looking for. "That kid deserves to be knighted," he murmured against her throat.

He brought them together with a sure, gentle thrust of his hips and Kailin sighed, knowing that those eleven years had been merely an eye blink of time, and that things were finally the way they should be. How long it lasted, she didn't know. She was so lost to the magic of Brett's lovemaking that time and the world vanished and there was no reality beyond the lean male body locked with hers, the growing tension that sought release. It caught her in a giant upsurge of pleasure so fierce that it made her cry out and she was only dimly aware of Brett's body arching into hers with sudden, fierce urgency. He went motionless, not even breathing, and she cradled him until the tension eased and he relaxed into her arms, panting and wet.

Finally Brett stirred, smiling sleepily down at her. He felt contented and impossibly happy, and wondered how he'd ever thought he could live without this woman. "Still think it's impossible to make love in a pickup truck?"

"You've done this before," she murmured accusingly.

"The trick's not to hit the gearshift and knock it into neutral," he said with a grin. "I had a friend once who parked on a down slope leading to a lake. He fell off the seat at a critical moment and got jammed against the gearshift level. When he tried to get up, he popped it into neutral and they wound up in three feet of water before the truck stopped."

Kailin sputtered with laughter, caressing his back and shoulders lazily. "I don't believe this. I haven't done anything so impetuous and crazy since—"

"The last time we were together," he finished for her, feeling ridiculously pleased with himself. It was intensely satisfying, if a little selfish, to think that there had been no one else in those eleven years who had made her laugh like this, had made her glow with such happiness.

"You're right." She kissed his shoulder. "You're good for me, Brett Douglass. You always were."

"I'm perfect for you. I just wish it hadn't taken us so long to figure it out."

"Maybe we needed that time," Kailin mused, drawing spirals on his back with her finger. "If we'd stayed together back then, who knows how long it would have lasted? We both needed to grow up."

"Who knows?" Brett said with a sigh. "I just know I'm never going to let you get away from me again."

"That sounds all very medieval and proprietary."

"Maybe they had it right all along. There was a time that when a man took a woman's virginity, he owned her." He gazed down at her slyly, waiting for the explosion.

He didn't have to wait long. "Took?" She gave him a poke in the ribs. "Virginity, you barbarian, is a gift a woman *gives* to a man. It's a symbol of her trust and commitment and love."

"There are still plenty of places in the world where it's no more than a commodity," he reminded her. "Just like a cow or a bushel of corn. A father uses his daughter's virginity as collateral to negotiate political or financial alliances. Without that leverage, she's just a liability."

As soon as he'd said it, Brett could have kicked himself. It hit just a little too close to home, and Kailin went quiet and still. Not saying anything, he simply held her tightly, kissing the top of her head.

They lay like that for an eternity, all wrapped up in a tangle of arms and legs and half-discarded clothing, until Kailin drowsily realized that it had stopped raining. The windows were still foggy with condensation, but the gray blur outside was lighter than it had been, a fact that Brett had been trying to ignore.

"I hate to mention this," she murmured, "but I think we'd better get upright and respectable before we shock some innocent passerby and start a major scandal."

"Do we have to?" His arms tightened around her, holding her firmly captive.

"Mmm." She kissed his ear with a regretful sigh. "I'd hate one of your local lovelies to spot your truck and drop by to see if the good doctor is in."

"The good doctor is in," he said with a salacious chuckle, moving his hips lightly. Then he gave a groan of protest and eased himself free of her, sitting up so they could untangle their legs. "These," he said, holding up a sodden lump of pink fabric, "are yours."

Kailin took her wet, cold panties and started wriggling into them.

Brett helpfully tugged up the top of her sundress, then rearranged his jeans and zippered them. He retrieved his sopping sweatshirt from the steering column and eyed it distastefully. "How would you like to spend the rest of the afternoon in front of a fire with a snifter of good brandy?"

"And a hot bath." Kailin ran her fingers through her wet, tangled hair. "I'd kill for a hot bath."

"Becky's staying with the McAllisters."

Kailin's mouth curved with a smile. "That's right."

"So," Brett breathed, wrapping his arms around her and nuzzling her neck, "there's no need for you to go home tonight, is there?"

"Dry clothes would be nice."

"You don't need any clothes for what I had in mind." He bit her earlobe gently. "I want to take you home and peel you out of that sundress and get so deep inside you again that it'll take us a week just to catch our breath. And I want to stay that way until morning."

"My-my car. It's here somewhere."

"We'll pick it up tomorrow."

"Becky... I have to tell Becky where I am."

"Call her from my place." Then he looked at her. "Is it going to be a problem? For her, I mean."

Kailin smiled. "No. I've told her about you."

It startled him. "You have?"

"I've told her we used to date."

Kailin frowned, seeming suddenly pensive, and Brett swallowed a sigh, knowing what she was thinking. She hadn't told Becky the truth—that *he* and not Royce was her father. It saddened him slightly, but he could see why she'd done it. She'd had no idea they would ever find each other again. As far as Becky was concerned, Royce *was* her father. He'd been there when she'd been born, he'd watched her grow up.

He wrenched his mind from the thought, concentrating instead on easing the truck through the lines of parked vehicles toward the exit. It was hard to get used to. What did he know about being a father, anyway? He glanced at Kailin, but she was staring out the side window, frowning thoughtfully.

She turned just then and saw him looking at her and smiled. "Besides, kids aren't as naive as we'd like to think. She told me a couple of months ago that she thought I should have a boyfriend."

"She *what*?" Brett nearly ran into the back of a parked van.

"She said she wasn't ready to deal with my getting married again—she didn't want to have to break in a new father just yet, was how she put it—but she didn't think it was fair for me to have to limit my social life because of that. She was even ready to help me pick him out."

"Did you take her up on it?" he asked very casually.

Kailin's mouth turned up. "Awfully nosy, aren't you?" Brett gave her a worried look and she laughed, curling up beside him and resting her head on his shoulder. "No, I didn't take her up on it. I think she has her eye on you as a likely candidate, though, so don't be surprised if you find yourself targeted for some very determined matchmaking."

"She won't get any argument from me," Brett assured her with a grin, squeezing her thigh gently. "I intend to do some serious work in that direction myself, starting in about half an hour."

"Half an hour?" Kailin's voice caught as his hand moved.

"It takes about half an hour to get up to my place," he said, massaging her leg. "Unless we hit a traffic jam."

Kailin let her eyes slide closed and covered his gently questing hand with hers. "Let's not hit any traffic jams," she whispered. "Brett, what are you doing?"

"Preliminaries," he said with a smoky laugh. "Just a few preliminaries."

To his relief they didn't run into any traffic jams until they reached the wide concrete bridge over Blind Pass. The highway crew still had barricades set up on the far end, reducing traffic to one lane, and Brett swore in quiet resignation as the young, sun-bronzed flagman stopped the car just ahead and motioned it to one side. Brett pulled in behind it and cut the engine.

He draped an arm over the steering wheel and gazed at the water spread out on either side of them. To their left lay the Gulf of Mexico, the lightly rippled surface as bright as hot silver in the lowering sun. The sky there was lightly brushed with crimson cloud, the sun itself a swollen red balloon. To their right lay what looked like a river, clear and blue, the banks lined with heavy green brush. Wide sandbars thrust out into the water, rising like smooth, beached whales.

"What are those people doing down there?" Kailin peered down at the handful of adults and children prowling the sand.

"Looking for shells. Sanibel is one of the three best shelling beaches in the world."

"That's what Craig was saying. In fact, they mention that in the brochures on Paradise Point." She turned to look at him. "He also says you're trying to stop the shelling."

"I'm not trying to stop anything," Brett said patiently. "I *am* trying to convince the local businesses to put more effort into educating the tourists about the ecological damage they're doing by taking live shells off the beach. Theoretically you're not allowed to take more than two live specimens per species per person—but I've seen people come off the beach with buckets full of live shells and starfish. They put them in the car and forget about them, and halfway between here and Chicago they wonder what the stink is and dump the rotting shells out onto the roadside. Or they clean them and take them home with great plans of getting into shellcraft, then get interested in something else and the shells get thrown out in a couple of years." He shook his head. "I hate waste."

Kailin smiled and braided her fingers with his, looking back down at the shellers. They were all wandering along in a curious bent-over shuffle, peering at the sand at their feet, and Kailin laughed. "It makes my back ache just watching them."

"It's called the Sanibel Stoop, and our local chiropractor does a booming business in high tourist season." He gestured to the dense greenery beyond the shellers. "That's all mangrove swamp out there. And Paradise Point."

"I know. I asked Craig to drive me out here yesterday after the meeting."

Brett looked at her sharply. "He drove you into the site?"

"We couldn't get in. The storm blew two big trees down across the access road, and they haven't gotten them moved yet." She looked out the other window at the Gulf. "He said there used to be a sandbar across there, but the storm blew it out, too."

He nodded to the far end of the bridge. "Last week's storm took out half the beach and undercut the bridge pilings. That's what the highway people are working on."

The flagman appeared just then. Brett started the truck, and they made their way slowly across. "What happens if a major hurricane hits?" Kailin asked suddenly. "Sanibel is wall-to-wall condominiums, most of them right out on the beach. If last week's storm could do this much damage..."

"It's a risk you take to live in Paradise," Brett replied quietly. "The hurricane of 1926 flooded the entire island and there have been some since that have done a lot of damage." He looked at her, smiling. "Thinking of telling the Paradise Point investors they'd be better off putting their money into pork belly futures?"

"About the same risk as far as I'm concerned," she said with a chuckle, "but my job's mediation, not investment counseling. They can put their money into snake oil for all I care."

"With Craig Bryant as the original snake-oil salesman." Kailin gave him an impatient look, and Brett laughed, squeezing her fingers. "Okay, okay, I'll lay off. Hell, I'm feeling so benevolent maybe I'll even pressure Zac into voting approval for Phase Three."

Even as he said it, Brett felt a twinge of doubt. It was just a fleeting thing, but it left a shadow that dispelled some of his ebullience. He stared thoughtfully at the traffic ahead of them. This wasn't any good, he thought. He'd made a decision this afternoon to let Kailin back into his heart again and he couldn't spend the rest of his life worrying about her motives. She'd made love with him today because she'd felt the same magic he had, not for any ulterior motive regarding Paradise Point. He had to believe that. Because if he ever stopped believing it, he had nothing left.

"Isn't that beautiful?" Kailin was leaning forward, gazing at the setting sun. It had set the cloud-quilted sky aflame, and even the restless Gulf seemed lighted by some inner fire.

The narrow, winding road ran right alongside the water here, flanked on either side with huge Australian pines, their lacy foliage meeting over the road in a delicate filigreed arch. A squadron of big brown pelicans swept low across the water in tight formation, wingtip to wingtip, then settled on the broken pilings of an old dock.

The road finally turned inland and wound into the small community of Captiva. It was so heavily wooded that most of the houses themselves were barely visible. Narrow, unmarked laneways ran off into apparent wilderness on either side, and when Brett finally turned left into what at first glance looked like a solid thicket of trees, Kailin looked at him in surprise.

The lane went through the palms and sprawling sea grape toward the Gulf. When they finally broke through into the clearing on the edge of the beach, Kailin gave a gasp of delight. The house wasn't large, but Brett had loved it from the moment he'd set eyes on it eight years ago. Like most of the homes on the islands, it was built up on pilings, as much for coolness as for protection against high water. The rough wood siding was worn soft and mellow by wind and sun, and it fit into the landscape of sand and tropical foliage as though it had grown there. Beyond it, out past the broad band of sea oats and the white sand beach, the restless Gulf was swallowing the last crescent of sun in a conflagration of color.

"No wonder you never come back to Indiana," Kailin said with a laugh. "If I lived here, I'd never leave the house."

"Take a good look." Brett slipped his arms around her and pulled her close to him, kissing the side of her throat. "Because I'm not letting you out of my bed for the next eighteen hours."

"You *are* turning medieval." Kailin reached up to grab a fistful of his hair and tugged it gently. "You sound like Bluebeard."

"The island of Captiva gets its name from the Spanish word *cautiva*—meaning captive," he murmured against her ear. "Back when pirates like Gasparilla and Black Caesar controlled these islands, if they found the wife or daughter of a wealthy family aboard any ship they plundered, they kept her for ransom. The women were supposedly kept here on Captiva until satisfactory business arrangements could be made . . . or for a few weeks of pleasure, as the case may be. It was known as La Isla de los Cautivas: the Island of Captives."

Kailin gave a muffled gasp of laughter and caught his straying hands. "And you think my father would pay a ransom for my return, do you?"

Brett grinned, reveling in having her in his arms again, heady with the feel and scent and taste of her. He bent down and scooped her up in his arms and started striding toward the house. "Ransom, hell—I wasn't even planning on asking." He smiled down at her, his heart soaring. "It was the plundering part I had in mind, sweet captive. And maybe a touch or two of pillage." Although who was the captive, he found himself wondering dazedly, and who the captor? And as for a ransom . . . well, what price his heart?

Seven

Kailin awoke to find herself alone in Brett's big bed. She smiled and stretched lazily, knowing she should get up but not remotely interested in doing so. In fact, she admitted with a contented smile, she would be perfectly happy to spend the rest of her life here.

Yawning, she nestled down into the tangled nest of bedding again. The evocative scent of their lovemaking still clung to the sheets, and Kailin smiled. She and Brett hadn't been out of this bed for more than a hour since he'd brought her here. They'd made love until they'd been so exhausted they'd fallen asleep in each other's arms, then awakened to make love again.

And again. Kailin's smile widened. They hadn't been able to get enough of each other, each exquisite encounter seeming to fuel rather than quench the fires within. It had been like this eleven years ago, she recalled sleepily. Pure magic!

Yawning again, she crawled out of bed and rummaged around in Brett's closet until she found a thick terry robe.

Then, combing her hair with her fingers, she staggered downstairs, still more asleep than awake.

Brett was leaning over the counter in the airy, bright kitchen, sipping a cup of coffee and reading a newspaper. He looked up when she stumbled in and grinned broadly. "I was just thinking of going up to see if you were still breathing."

"Coffee," she croaked. "Please, coffee..."

"Are you still a zombie in the morning until you've had your caffeine?" He patted her gently on the bottom, then poured her a generous mugful and set it in front of her. "Drink."

"Mmm." Kailin locked both hands around the mug and lifted it to her mouth. Brett gave a snort of laughter and shook his head. Then, to her everlasting gratitude, he went back to his own coffee and the paper and left her in peace.

"Thank you," she said a few minutes later, taking a deep breath and looking around her for the first time.

"Anytime. Want another cup?"

She shook her head. "I mean for not talking. I can't stand people who roll out of bed at the crack of dawn all chipper and full of good spirits."

Brett laughed. "I don't think 9:30 is considered the crack of dawn."

"It is when you didn't get any sleep the night before."

"We didn't, did we?" His smile was warm and lazy.

Kailin looked up at him through the steam from her coffee, feeling a familiar little quiver settle low in her stomach. He was lounging lazily against the counter, naked except for a towel wrapped rather haphazardly around his hips, and he looked decidedly and appealingly male. There was something in the way he was looking at her that made her feel sleepy and warm and she smiled, gazing at him through half-lowered lashes. "What are you thinking about?"

He held his hand out, smiling, and Kailin got up and walked across to him. She set the coffee aside and ran her hands across his broad chest, leaned forward to kiss his shoulder, moving her lips lightly to the hollow in his throat.

"This is ridiculous," she whispered, gliding her hands up his smooth, muscled back. "Do you suppose we're normal? I mean, we made love all night long. Then when we got up the first time this morning, all you had to do was look at me and..."

Brett chuckled. "Some people jog every morning, some people do calisthenics, some people—"

"Most people do not make love on the stairs as they're going down to make breakfast," she reminded him with a laugh. "This is crazy, you have to admit it."

"I'm not admitting anything except that I can't get enough of you." He smoothed her hair back and kissed the end of her nose. "I have to go down to the clinic for a while, but I'll try to get away for a couple of hours. Be here for me?"

Kailin smiled. "I'd love to, but I have to get home. I promised Becky that we'd take a boat tour around the islands today. She's dying to go scuba diving."

"I have a sailboat," he whispered coaxingly. "The *Sweet Retreat*, docked near here. I have a friend in Fort Myers Beach who owes me a favor. I could talk him into taking over at the clinic while we spend a week or more exploring all the little coves and inlets and beaches...."

"And I have a job to do, remember?" she reminded him with a laugh. "I've got to work up a list of recommendations regarding Paradise Point before the next meeting, and that means reviewing your committee's report and talking with Craig Bryant again."

"Bryant?" Brett's brows pulled together.

"Yes, Bryant," Kailin said tolerantly. "I'm supposed to be getting both sides of this, remember? Though heaven knows I think I've compromised my impartiality a bit."

"A number of times," Brett purred, eyes glowing. "And I intend to ensure that we compromise it regularly from now on."

Kailin smiled and rested her cheek on Brett's chest, listening to the strong, regular beat of his heart. And when the Paradise Point project was over and she had to go home? They hadn't talked about that last night. They hadn't talked about anything but the present, as though the past and future didn't even exist. Maybe in a way they didn't, Kailin decided thoughtfully. Maybe it was better if they just went on like this for a while, locked in the magic of *now*, letting the past heal and the future wait.

"You going to fix me breakfast?" she asked, smiling up at him. At his assent, she stood on tiptoe to plant a kiss full on his mouth. "Be down in a jiffy."

Kailin heard the angry voices before she was even out of the shower. One was Brett's, the other an indistinct mutter. She toweled herself dry, then slipped on the robe and belted it as she walked back into the bedroom. There was a scuffle just outside the bedroom door, a snarl of profanity, then the door flew inward and two men burst into the room.

"Craig!" Kailin stared at Craig Bryant in astonishment.

He glowered across the rumpled bed at her, breathing heavily. His face was flushed and the front of his shirt crumpled as though someone had grabbed a fistful of the fabric. "I've been looking for you since yesterday afternoon," he said angrily. "I should have guessed you'd be here. Douglass was panting after you like a—"

"One more word out of you, Bryant," Brett said, "and you're going to be missing some teeth."

"Save your breath for your court appearance, Douglass!" Craig waved a handful of papers in the air. "I know why you and your committee have been blocking Phase Three of Paradise Point. It's all here in black and white!"

"What are you talking about?"

"TexAm Construction," Craig stated triumphantly. "You didn't think I'd find out, did you?"

"Where did you get that information?" Brett's eyes glowed dangerously, and he took a step toward Craig.

Craig smiled. "I'm going to crucify you, Douglass. Collusion with intent to defraud, for a start. By the time I'm finished with you, your little committee's going to be facing enough charges to put you—"

"What are you talking about, Craig?" Kailin snapped.

Craig's angry gaze swung around to her. "I'm talking about a sweet little deal lover boy here has cooked up with TexAm Construction to push Gulf Coast into bankruptcy. With us out of the way, TexAm can step in and pick up the property for a song. But I guess you'd know all about that, wouldn't you?" He let his eyes wander over her. "Looks like the good chairman hasn't wasted any time in making sure what side of the fence you're on."

A hot flush spread across Kailin's cheeks, but she tipped her chin up and stared at Craig without flinching. "Mr. Douglass and I have known each other for years. Our relationship doesn't concern you, the Land Use Committee *or* Gulf Coast."

"Like hell. I've never known a woman yet who could take a tumble through a man's bed, then face the guy across a boardroom table as though nothing happened. Or is this how you big-city girls do business?"

Brett growled something and took two strides towards Craig. Craig threw up his hands. "Hey, no problem. I'm leaving."

"Damn right you are," Brett grabbed the back of Craig's jacket and shoved him toward the door. "The only question is whether you're leaving in one piece."

Craig paused by the door and turned to look at Kailin. "Just in case he's got you conned, too, baby, read this." He threw the wad of crumpled papers onto the bed. Then, with one last look at Brett, he shrugged his shoulders to settle his jacket and strode out the door and down the stairs.

Kailin looked at Brett angrily. "Thanks. I really enjoyed that." She snatched up her panties and pulled them on, then tossed the robe aside and slipped into her sundress, too annoyed to even care that Brett was watching. "Next time you hold a meeting in your bedroom, I'd appreciate a bit of warning. My work is difficult enough without everyone discovering I'm sleeping with one of the parties involved."

"Maybe you should have thought of that yesterday afternoon," Brett snapped back, moving his shoulders as though to loosen tight muscles. He prowled the bedroom like something caged, large and angry and restless.

Kailin had her mouth open to fire back an angry retort, then eased her breath out and subsided. "You're right," she said quietly. "I'm sorry. I knew what I was doing." She smiled tentatively. "For what it's worth, I'd do it again."

Brett stared at her for a moment, and then his own mouth lifted with a faint, wry smile. "Promise?"

"Is that what you want?" she asked seriously.

"Yes. It's very much what I want."

Kailin sighed and ran her fingers through her tangled hair, tossing it back from her face. "You do realize, don't you, that this—" she gestured toward the bed "—can't have any effect on my job? I'm not going to sleep with you and sell Gulf Coast out because of it."

"What you and I have here," Brett replied softly, "doesn't have a damned thing to do with Gulf Coast. This has got to do with eleven years ago, and a lot of dreams gone wrong. This is our second chance, Kailin." He walked across and folded his arms around her, kissing the top of her head. "I gotta go, kid," he murmured regretfully. "Kathy will be wondering if I've finally made good my threat to toss it all over and become a beach bum if I don't get down there pretty soon. I called a buddy of mine and had him bring your car up—he dropped it off while you were in the shower.

And I left your breakfast on the table. There's an extra house key there, too. I'd like to think you'll be here tonight."

"If I can. But I don't want to farm Becky out with the McAllisters every night just so I can stay here. It's the only vacation we've had together in months, and she has to leave for Indiana in another week."

"She can stay here. There's an extra bedroom."

Kailin frowned slightly, shaking her head. "I don't think she's ready for that yet, Brett. And I guess I'm not, either." She toyed with a button on his shirt, not meeting his eyes. "I've dated a bit since Royce died, but I've never... gotten close to anyone. This kind of close." She looked up at him. "I have to be very sure before I bring a man into Becky's life too, Brett."

"I'm not just passing through, Kailin," he said quietly. He ran the back of his hand down her cheek, his eyes searching hers. "Not this time, by God."

Kailin's heart did a slow cartwheel, and she felt something within her pull so tight it almost hurt. She touched his cheek, wondering if he could read the love in her eyes, then smiled and turned her face to kiss his fingers. "Go. You have a veterinary practice to run. I'll call you when Becky and I get back from our boat ride—we can have dinner together, anyway. Becky's quite proud of the fact she doesn't need a baby-sitter anymore, and the people in the next condo are marvelous, so I don't worry about her being alone for a few hours." She laughed. "She'll make a bushel of popcorn and watch *Top Gun* for the umpteenth time and wish I went out more often."

Brett glanced at the clock, then swore under his breath and kissed her swiftly. He picked up his denim jacket, grinning over his shoulder as he headed for the door. "See you tonight, sweetheart. We'll have dinner here—steak, wine and each other. That sound okay?"

"That sounds perfect." Kailin's laughter rose through the spangled sunlight, and as she listened to Brett gallop down the stairs she felt like shouting with sheer happiness. It was going to work out after all, she thought with pleasure. It was really going to work out this time.

"Is he gonna be okay, Dr. Douglass?" The little boy standing at the end of the examining table wiped one grubby fist across his cheek, smearing tears and dirt. His chin wobbled and he swallowed, gazing tearfully up at the small shaggy dog lying quietly under Brett's probing hands.

"He'll be okay," Brett assured him gently, still examining the dog. It whimpered and rolled its eyes to look at him, shivering so badly the tags on its collar tinkled like bells.

"Oh, thank goodness." The young woman standing by the door closed her eyes in relief. "Joey's usually so careful with Hobo. I've told him not to walk along that stretch of highway, but—" She shrugged helplessly, looking down at her son.

"I won't ever take him there again," Joey sobbed. "I promise, Mom. Honest, I won't." He wiped his face with the back of his hand and stepped nearer the table. "I'm sorry, Hobo."

Brett traded a smile with the woman, noticing that she was having trouble keeping her own tears from spilling. He nodded toward the small desk beside her. "Tissues in the top right drawer, Helen."

She gave a wet laugh and pulled out a handful of tissues and dabbed her eyes. "When Joey came running into the house carrying Hobo, both of them covered with blood and howling their heads off, it scared me half to death!"

"Well, he's one lucky pup." Brett lifted the small dog down and put him gently in Joey's outstretched arms.

"Thank you, Dr. Douglass." Joey smiled up at Brett radiantly.

"From the heart!" His mother laughed and dabbed at her eyes again. "You know I'll pay you something just as soon as Jim's arm is better and he can go back to work."

"Don't worry about it, Helen." Brett turned the water on in the small sink and started lathering his hands with soap. "When Jim's working again, tell him to drop off a pail of shrimp and we'll call it even."

Her face broke into a smile almost as radiant as her son's. "I'll send Joey around tomorrow with a basket of preserves and a couple of apple pies." Then, before Brett could protest, she turned and hurried after her son.

"Apple pies," Kathy said a few minutes later. She eyed Brett's trim midriff speculatively. "Last week it was Carla Mason's strawberry jam. And before that, Tilly Kuzack's black forest cake."

Brett grinned at her. "It's a hell of a life, but hey—someone's got to do it."

"Right," Kathy drawled. "You've got company, by the way." She smiled again, one eyebrow lifting. "Very pretty, and very mad."

Brett winced. "Now what? Who?"

"Me." They both wheeled around as the door to the surgery slammed open and Kailin strode into the room, practically trailing smoke. "And I want to know just what the *hell* you think you're doing."

Kathy eased herself from between them. "I'll clean up in here later," she said to no one in particular. "I think I hear the phone ringing." And with that she was gone, closing the door softly behind her.

Brett looked at Kailin. The two tall stained-glass windows, the only remnants of the building's previous life, spilled a rainbow of light behind her, turning her golden hair to flame. But it wasn't her hair that caught Brett's attention—it was her eyes, wide and bright and snapping with anger. "Hi. I thought you and Becky were going—"

She strode across the room and threw a sheaf of papers onto the operating table. "Would you like to tell me what's going on?"

Brett looked at the papers, slowly realizing that they were the ones Craig Bryant had been waving around that morning. "It's not all that complicated. TexAm Construction is a land development corporation headquartered in Houston. They came to us a few months ago about buying property on Captiva and Sanibel. What's the problem?"

"The problem," she said evenly, "is that your committee is coming this close—" she held her two fingers so close together that Brett couldn't even see daylight between them "—*this* close, mister, to outright fraud. Craig Bryant was right this morning—he *could* take you to court on a collusion charge. I doubt he'd manage to pull it off, but he could tie you up in court for the next twenty years!" The last two words ricocheted off the walls, and she stopped, breathing heavily. "Damn it, Brett, how could you be so careless?"

"What the hell are you talking about?" Brett threw the papers down, eyeing her impatiently.

"I am talking about a breach of every antitrust regulation in the country, that's what I'm talking about." Her eyes glittered in the rainbowed light from the windows. "Gulf Coast is sitting on land that TexAm wants. The Gulf Coast project is in trouble, but you're committed. *Unless* Gulf Coast goes bankrupt. Then TexAm can step in, buying up Paradise Point at five cents on the dollar, and everyone's happy. Except Gulf Coast."

"It's a tough business," Brett reminded her.

"Yeah, it sure is." Kailin strode across in front of him and back again, cheeks flushed.

"TexAm hasn't made a firm offer on anything. It's no big deal."

"No big deal." She planted herself in front of him, hands on trim hips. "The resort they're proposing is nearly twice the size of Paradise Point, which is odd, considering you

forced Gulf Coast to downsize their original projections by
a third. But the really interesting part is that TexAm prom-
ises to donate a huge tract of wetlands back to Sanibel for a
wildlife and bird preserve.''

"So?" Brett felt his temper start to rise in spite of his best
efforts.

Kailin stared at him as though she didn't believe what she
was hearing. "It's bribery, Brett. Simple, old-fashioned
bribery."

"What are you talking about?" Brett demanded.
"TexAm came to us with that offer after it was apparent
Gulf Coast was in trouble. If Gulf Coast *does* go down,
we're going to be stuck with a half-finished condo development with enough liens and writs against it to sink the
entire islands. There aren't many developers willing to take
over a mess like that."

"And even fewer," Kailin said silkily, "who'd be willing
to deed half of it back as a conservation area. All the committee has to do to get that tract of land is to stonewall Gulf
Coast's attempts to salvage Paradise Point. Once they've
gone down the tubes, the bank will be only too happy to sell
the Point off at whatever they can get for it." She took a step
toward him. "Except TexAm couldn't possibly know how
much trouble Gulf Coast is in unless someone told them."

"Are you saying that I—?" Brett yelped.

"I'm saying the whole thing stinks of collusion and bribery. Whether it was intentional or not, I don't know— I'm
willing to give you the benefit of the doubt. But no government probe sent down here to investigate would be that
generous." She turned and strode across the room from
him, heels clicking on the polished floor. "If it's so innocent, why didn't you tell me about it? Why wasn't it tabled
at the meeting?"

"I didn't tell you about it because it hasn't got anything
to do with you," Brett told her bluntly. "Your job is to ne-

gotiate an understanding between us and Gulf Coast. That's all. TexAm hasn't got a damned thing to do with either."

"It's got everything to do with it!" Kailin turned to glare at him. "I *am* trying to do my job, Brett. That's to sort out this mess so everyone comes out a winner—you, the investors, Gulf Coast. But I'm not going to be able to do that job if you and your committee are sneaking around making deals behind my back. It's not just unfair, it's unethical!"

"Unethical?" Brett's bellow made Kailin blink. He pushed himself away from the desk. "If we're going to talk ethics, lady, let's talk about the ethics of using cut-rate building materials to skim a profit during construction."

"What do you mean?"

"Why don't you ask your good friend Craig Bryant?"

"You're making a serious allegation, Brett."

"Which can be proved by an on-site inspection of Phase Two. Or what's left of it."

Kailin stood looking at him for a long while. "Craig's already admitted that Phase Two suffered some damage in last week's storm. That's to be expected, considering the place was still under construction and especially vulnerable. The storm was one step below a full-fledged hurricane."

"Phase Two is—was—over ninety percent complete, and as solid as it was ever going to be. It didn't suffer 'some damage,' it was damned near totaled. Nothing can explain the extent of the destruction but lousy workmanship, substandard materials and a lot of cut corners." Brett let her think about that for a moment, knowing by her expression that she was taking in every word. She was too good at her job *not* to be thinking about the possibilities. "*Someone,*" he added softly, "made a lot of under-the-table money on that project."

Her eyes narrowed. "What you're suggesting isn't just unethical, it's grounds for a criminal action suit. Craig might play close to the line sometimes, but he's not that stupid.''

"Don't be so innocent. You know how the game is played. Hell, you were weaned on Monopoly. Anything goes in big business as long as you don't get caught, you know that.''

"And you don't?" Kailin's eyebrow arched delicately. "St. Douglass the Pure, my father used to call you. He'd have a fit if he could see you now, playing at big business like an old pro. When you told me you'd mellowed, I didn't realize you meant you'd sold out.''

The tenuous hold that Brett had managed to keep on his temper very nearly snapped. "I have *not* sold out!"

"No?" Kailin stared at him defiantly. "Everyone knows how hard you've been fighting to get more wetlands put aside as natural habitat areas, Brett. You've been one of the leaders in the conservation movement down here for years. If Gulf Coast loses Paradise Point and TexAm picks it up, you'll get that tract of swamp—even though it means approving a bigger development than originally planned. Now *I* call that a sellout.''

"Give a little, get a little," Brett growled. "I learned years ago that you can't have it all your own way all the time." He caught the anger, swallowed it. "And no one is sneaking around behind your back—no one from *my* side of the table, anyway.''

"And just what is *that* supposed to mean?''

"If Gulf Coast goes bankrupt, the Bryant family is going to be hurting—and I can't see Craig Bryant giving it all up without a fight. I wouldn't put it past him to deal from both sides of the deck and work a deal with TexAm—inside information for hard, cold cash.''

"Come on, Brett. That makes even less sense than—''

"Than what?" Brett asked angrily. "Than my selling out?''

"Exactly!''

"You think so?" Brett gave a snort of harsh laughter. "Craig Bryant is like an iceberg, Kailin—you only see what he wants you to see. Or maybe the sellout isn't on Bryant's side of the table at all."

Kailin stared at him blankly. "What are you saying?"

"I don't know what I'm saying," he replied with quiet intensity, wishing with every atom that he could shake free of the suspicion. "It's just that I keep asking myself why, of all the people in the world, you're the one looking at me across that meeting table, Kailin. Coincidence? Fate? Or is there more to it?"

"Such as?" She had gone pale, her eyes very wide. "You think that I'm working with Craig Bryant to..." She gestured helplessly, as though at a loss for words.

"The two of you seem to know each other pretty well." He hadn't intended to say it, but the words were out before he could stop them, rancid with suspicion. He stared at her, daring her to deny it, something aching deep and cold within him. "I just keep wondering if—"

"If he's using me to manipulate you," she completed. "That possibility didn't seem to bother you much yesterday afternoon. Or last night. Or maybe *you* were using me. Was I picking your brains last night, or were you picking mine? Am I Craig's pawn or yours? Or am I playing both ends against the middle for some devious little purpose of my own?"

Damn it, that wasn't what he'd meant at all! Or was it? Brett rubbed his forehead, trying to ease a dull throb that had settled there in the past few minutes. It was all falling apart, disappearing through his fingers like smoke, and he didn't even know how to stop it. "Kailin..."

"You think I'm using you just like you believed I used you before, don't you?" she whispered. "You didn't believe I loved you then. You didn't even believe I was pregnant. I used to lie awake at night trying to convince myself that you hadn't taken that money, that you'd come riding up in that old MGB and we'd go off together."

"I didn't take the money," Brett said angrily.

"No, but you didn't exactly knock yourself out trying to find me, either."

"Your father—!"

"My father was just a man, Brett. He couldn't have kept you away from me if you'd really tried." She gazed at him, a flash of what might have been tears in her eyes. "I guess you decided that being saddled with a wife and baby didn't fit your plans."

"Like being married to me didn't fit yours?" he retorted. Her accusation had stung, and he could feel his temper flaring again. "Stop kidding yourself about who ran out on whom, Kailin. You're the one who married Royce McGuire and let him raise my daughter."

"She's not your daughter!" Kailin shouted, then stared at him as though the words were as great a shock to her as they were to him.

Eight

—

Brett felt an eerie coolness drift through the room. "What did you say?" he asked very softly.

He thought he heard her sigh. When she slowly turned and looked at him, her face was bleak. "This isn't how I wanted to tell you, Brett, but it's true. Becky is Royce's daughter, not yours. I—I lost yours."

"Lost...it?" Brett heard the words but didn't recognize the voice as his own. He shook his head, as though that could somehow make all this come clear. "How do you lose a baby, Kailin?" he asked very reasonably. "They're not like umbrellas and old shoes. You don't just put them down one day and forget where you left them."

"I had a miscarriage nine days after Royce and I were married."

"You were on your honeymoon nine days after you were married." It was a ridiculous thing to say, as though a honeymoon somehow made a miscarriage impossible, but it was like a talisman, protecting him, and he clung to it fiercely.

"Quebec City, Canada. The Château Frontenac hotel." She was staring at him with such an odd expression that he added unnecessarily, "I didn't believe you'd married him until I...checked." He took a deep breath. "Look, just what kind of game are you playing, Kailin? Becky for Paradise Point, is that it? If I don't swing the committee over to approve Phase Three, I'll never see my daughter again?"

Kailin had gone ghost-white. "My God," she whispered, "what do you think I am?"

"Your father's daughter." He smiled bitterly and walked back to the desk. How could it have gone so wrong? He'd been so sure this morning, so positive that *this* time it was going to be all right, that *this* time they were going to have the happiness they'd only been promised eleven years ago.

She was staring at him with a look of such unutterable hurt on her face that for the briefest moment he wondered if he'd been wrong. But he caught himself as in the next instant that closed, remote mask shuttered over her face again. She gazed at him for a long moment, those moss-green eyes impossible to read, then turned and walked to the door.

"Kailin?" The word was torn from him.

"What?" She paused with her hand on the knob, not turning to look at him.

"Was that the truth...about Becky?" He held his breath, wanting to know and at the same time dreading the answer. Hating her in that moment for making him ask.

Her back straightened. "I've never lied to you in my entire life, Brett. That was always the problem between us—you never even knew me well enough to understand that."

She was gone. Brett stared at the closing door numbly. He swallowed, aching with a soul-deep emptiness that was so bitterly familiar that it took him a moment to understand why.

Then he remembered. Eleven years ago he'd stood and watched a door swing slowly closed like that. And then, as now, he'd felt a part of himself twist free and vanish.

Kailin stood on the huge balcony of her rented apartment and stared unseeingly down at the beach. The unseasonably warm weather had brought the weekend sunseekers out in force, and the beach was a colorful mosaic of oiled bodies. It was an idyllic scene, and for a moment Kailin found herself hating them all.

She smiled. It had been a long while since she'd allowed herself to indulge in a bit of self-pity, and it felt oddly satisfying. Her father had never tolerated it. But then her father had rarely tolerated any sign of weakness. *Don't show them anything* had been his credo, and he'd taught her well. Only with Becky could she be real and spontaneous. Why, she asked herself idly, couldn't she just let go of all the programmed responses and let the real Kailin McGuire out? Was she that insecure and frightened?

Life hurts, her father had told her once. The trick is not to show it.

She'd hurt today.

Kailin closed her eyes for an instant, holding that remembered pain at bay by sheer force of will. Then, without even thinking about it, she relaxed the barriers and let it sweep over her, relishing its sting. Relishing *feeling*.

Pain. Anger. Frustration. They curdled together, and she didn't even bother stopping the tears. She could still hear Brett's voice. See the disbelief and the suspicion in his eyes. "What's the use?" she asked out loud. "Why don't you just go home and tell your father to find someone else to do his dirty work?"

But she couldn't go home. She'd given her word.

She stepped back into the cool bedroom and kicked her shoes off. They hit the closet door with a bang that startled Maverick so badly he wailed and scuttled for the safety of her ankles.

"Sorry, Mav," she whispered contritely, picking the kitten up and tucking him against her shoulder. "It was just a passing tantrum, nothing serious."

She stretched out on her bed and stared at the ceiling. Maverick bumped his head against her chin, then gnawed on the strap of her dress. She couldn't leave the Paradise Point investors high and dry when she'd given her word to sort this mess out; she couldn't leave Charlie Bryant high and dry, either. She'd felt sorry for the old man when she'd talked with him a month or more ago. His dreams of building a dynastic empire were crumbling around him, and it must have taken fantastic courage to tell her that his son was ruining Gulf Coast Developments.

What price an old man's pride? she found herself wondering. What had it cost her father to beg her to take on this job? What, for that matter, was it costing her?

Frowning, she thought of Brett's accusations about Craig and Paradise Point. He wouldn't be the first developer to make deals with his contractors. It was a simple scam, and it was usually impossible to detect. The building codes and blueprints would specify one thing—a certain size lumber to be used for floor supports, for instance, or a specific distance left between wall joists. The supply invoices would reflect what was specified, but in reality floors would be supported with two-by-eights instead of two-by-tens, wall joists would be set an extra two or three inches apart. If the scam was subtle enough, the contractor could get away with it. Only one buyer in ten thousand ever went into the basement and looked at the flooring in a new house; perhaps half of those knew what to look for.

But if the builder was too greedy, if the rip-offs were too flagrant, the structural integrity of the building itself was compromised. Bridges fell down; office towers collapsed halfway through construction; highways dissolved in the first heavy rain. It happened.

Had it happened on Phase Two of Paradise Point?

There was one way to find out. The first step was to go out there and see if the storm damage was as bad as Brett had said. The second was to bring in a building inspector and have him go over the place nail by nail. If everything was as it should be, his report would settle any doubts still harbored by Brett's Land Use Committee. If it *wasn't*....

"Well," she advised the sleeping kitten, "then we see just how good Kailin McGuire really is."

"I'm sorry, ma'am." The security guard shifted the wad of tobacco to his other cheek, then turned his head and spat tidily into the ditch. "But I can't let y'all in there. Rules."

It took Kailin every ounce of willpower to resist telling the man blocking her way precisely what he could do with his rules. Behind him lay the muddy dirt road leading into Phase Two of the Paradise Point resort complex, tantalizing in its nearness. Two massive trees lay across it just at the entrance, blocking it completely. Behind her lay Phase One, serene and quiet in the noonday sun, the picturesque adobe-style buildings and well-cared-for gardens a postcard version of what paradise should look like.

She drew in a deep, calming breath, and tried again. "Look, Craig Bryant is a friend and I'm working with him on the Paradise Point project. He told me I could come in here to look the site over." She was stretching the truth, but who cared?

"Sorry, ma'am." Calm gray eyes met her, as obdurate and unmoved by her pleas as stone. "No pass, no access, them's the rules." He shrugged a meaty shoulder toward the two trees. "Can't get in nohow."

"Look," Kailin snapped, all patience gone, "I know you're just doing your job, but I need to get on that site. Now if you call Craig's office, they'll tell you that I—"

"Can't do that, ma'am. Couldn't let Charlie Bryant hisself in without a pass." The human mountain smiled congenially. "'Sides, I couldn't let y'all in anyways. It's a construction site, and y'all need a hard hat—them's *government* rules."

"Fine." She turned on her heel and marched across to her rental car. Now what? Craig Bryant was out of town and his secretary at the Sanibel office had no idea where he was, when he'd be back, or even *if* he'd be back. Nor was she inclined to give Kailin a pass to get into Phase Two.

The security guard smiled amiably at her as she turned the car around, and she smiled back. I'll be back, she promised him silently. One way or another, I *will* be back.

There had to be another way.

Kailin draped her arms across the top of the steering wheel, then rested her chin on them and sighed heavily, staring out at the old church housing Brett's vet clinic. Except if there was, *she* couldn't think of it.

Asking Brett for help didn't mean he'd do it, though. In fact, he was just as likely to tell her to go to hell. Not that she could blame him. Kailin winced at the memory of his expression when she'd blurted out the truth about Becky. If she had deliberately set out to hurt him, she couldn't have chosen a more brutally effective method.

It was ironic in a way. Eleven years ago they'd argued over a baby he didn't believe existed, and two mornings ago he'd wanted desperately to believe that Becky *was* his.

And yet it was Brett alone who could get her what she needed. She took a deep breath, then pushed open the car door and stepped out.

"Come on in!" The disembodied female voice came from somewhere under the big desk in the waiting room.

The place had Brett Douglass written all over it, from the blue denim jacket tossed carelessly over the back of a chair to the pair of muddy work boots drying in the corner. There were a couple of battered filing cabinets on one side of the desk, the tops littered with paper, plants and old coffee cups.

A mop of curly brown hair popped up from behind the desk, and Kathy Fischer grinned broadly at her. "Hi!"

Kailin smiled. "Hi. I'm looking for Brett again, but no fireworks this time, I promise."

Kathy laughed and stood up, holding a squirming mass of fur. "He's out back." She leaned over and deposited a ferret into Kailin's hands. "Could you take the little pest out to Brett? Three of them got loose last night and we're moving them to an outside cage they'll *never* get open!"

It was as supple as a fur-covered spring, pausing long enough to sniff Kailin's fingers before trying to go in fifteen directions at once. It squeezed under her arm and found her open canvas shoulder bag and promptly disappeared into its depths.

Kailin found the door leading out to the backyard, full of cages and holding pens. Brett was at the far end, stripped to the waist, his broad back gleaming with sweat as he nailed the framework of another set of cages together with quick, competent blows of the hammer.

She stood in the doorway for a long moment until Brett glanced around. The hammering faltered, then stopped, and he stared at her in silence, eyes dark with surprise. But she could also read the wary suspicion of a man hurt once too often. The taut silence lengthened, and then Brett resumed his hammering, pounding the nails in with short, savage blows.

Great start. They hadn't even said anything yet, and he was already angry.

"I...um...tried to look at Phase Two this morning." Nothing. Not even a pause. Kailin stared at his strong, sunbronzed back in frustration. He wasn't going to give an inch, damn him.

Ill at ease, she looked at the array of wildlife in the pens: two opossums curled up in a knot, a small heron with its wing in a splint, a huge turtle sunning itself in a child's plastic wading pool, ignoring the three-legged alligator in the next cage.

"You've got quite a little menagerie out here," she said. "Are you taking up zookeeping or expecting a heavy rain?"

The hammering paused. She glanced around and found Brett watching her carefully, as though undecided about answering her. "No flood, no ark. Just strays that people bring in."

He spoke as though each word took an effort, and Kailin sighed. This was going to be tougher than she'd anticipated. "How did this alligator lose its leg?"

"Fight." The word was punctuated by hammer blows.

"For food?" Kailin managed to keep her growing irritation out of her voice. She could play this game as long as he could. Longer, if necessary.

"Sex." Brett straightened, his eyes holding hers challengingly. He wiped the sweat from his forehead with his arm.

"That will do it," Kailin said calmly. "So, did he get the lady?"

"No." Three sharp hammer blows. "She ran off with someone else while he and his opponent were battling for her favors."

"She'd probably have broken his heart anyway."

"Undoubtedly. Most women do."

Kailin swallowed a sigh and rested her forearms on the top of the turtle's cage, staring down at it. "Would it help if I said I was sorry?" she asked quietly.

The hammering faltered and stopped. "For what?" It sounded torn out of him, as though he were annoyed at himself for giving her even that much.

"For all of it," Kailin turned to look at him. "For letting you think Becky was your daughter for as long as I did. I never thought that you'd think she was, because it never occurred to me that you'd finally believed I was pregnant in the first place. I should have told you right at the beginning, but there... just didn't seem to be a good time. And I didn't realize it was... well, so important to you."

His eyes held hers, dark with some emotion Kailin couldn't even guess at. Then he turned his attention back to the cage. "Neither did I," he said gruffly, not looking at her.

Watching him, Kailin felt her heart ache. What had that admission cost him? she wondered sadly. What momentary dreams had the truth shattered? He glanced around. Their eyes caught and held, then he frowned fleetingly and looked away. Unrolling a large sheet of wire mesh, he stretched it across the wooden framework. Silently Kailin walked over and held it for him. Brett started nailing it down without saying a thing.

"Where do they all come from? The animals, I mean?"

"People bring them in." He waited for her to unroll more of the wire. "Anything that's injured, we mend it as best we can and turn it loose again." He gave his head an impatient shake. "Some days it's a losing battle."

You're a kind and gentle man, Brett Douglass, Kailin found herself thinking. Always out there standing up for the little guy, battling for good against impossible odds. Why did he find it so easy to love these small furred things yet so difficult to love her?

"What the hell—?"

Brett was staring at something behind her, and Kailin looked around. Her own eyes widened at the sight of her canvas carryall making its way clumsily across the yard, whirring and chattering as it went.

Kailin pounced on it, laughing, and hauled the rumpled ferret out. "I forgot all about you!"

Brett looked at her quizzically, then nodded toward the far set of cages. "Pop him with the others."

Pop wasn't quite the right word. Trying to stuff a ferret through a hole was like trying to stuff a sock full of marbles through the eye of a needle. The other two ferrets weren't helping the effort—they were just as intent on oozing out as Kailin was trying to get the third *in*. She finally managed to get them all more or less on the right side, and she closed the door, trying not to pinch too many toes, feeling like a drunk tank jailer on a Saturday night.

"You do that like a pro."

"Oh, I have talents you haven't even suspected yet." Brett looked at her sharply, but Kailin simply unrolled another length of wire. She stretched it across the cage frame, watching the play of muscle in his back as Brett worked, the bulge of his biceps, the fine peppering of dark hairs along his forearms.

He looked up just then, those blue eyes so close that it was like falling into deep water. The shock left her breathless and she simply stared at him. She could see the tiny beads of sweat on his upper lip, the almost imperceptible tightening of the skin around his eyes, and in that heartbeat eternity she knew he was going to kiss her.

He didn't. He closed his eyes instead and turned his head away, the muscles along his jaw throbbing as though he were clenching his teeth. Then he breathed an oath and stood up, his fingers, trailing fire where they brushed her arm, lingered for the briefest moment on her shoulder.

"You didn't come here to help build these cages," he said tightly.

He sounded resentful, even angry. So he was still fighting her. Fighting *himself*. Fighting everything he knew in his heart to be true but was too angry and stubborn to admit. "No," she said quietly. "I need your help." Silence answered her, fraught with tension. "I said, I—"

"I heard you. I'm just waiting for the catch."

"There is no catch. I've been trying to get into the Phase Two site for two days, but I'm being stonewalled. I'd hoped you could help me."

Surprise flared in his eyes, followed by frank curiosity. "What do you mean, stonewalled?"

"I called Craig Bryant a couple of hours after I . . . left your place." His eyes narrowed fractionally, but they gave Kailin no clue as to what he was thinking. "I told him that either I got an on-site inspection, trees or no trees, or I went straight to the top. He was quite agreeable to my going out there, but very...vague." She smiled humorlessly. "Since then he's been as elusive as a snake. I went out there yesterday, but they've got a security guard at the entrance I swear is a sumo wrestler in his spare time."

"What do you want me to do?"

"You were the one making all the accusations the other day. The least you can do is help me get in there to see for myself."

"Did you see the roots of those trees across the road?"

"No. No, I don't think I did," Kailin said, frowning thoughtfully.

"The only big trees growing along that road are Australian pine. When they go over, they pull up a huge circle of soil and roots. I suspect those trees have been cut and deliberately placed across the road to keep people out. Especially people like you."

"But why would anyone—?"

Her eyes widened, and Brett smiled. "If word gets out about how much damage that storm really did, Bryant's finished. Even he's not enough of a fast-talker to convince people it wasn't the result of substandard materials."

"Get me in there so *I* can see it."

"Why?" He held her gaze deliberately. "So you can write a report downplaying the damage?"

"So I can write a report detailing exactly what's been going on since Craig took over from his father." She held his stare challengingly. "You've accused me of being unfair, Brett, but you're ready to write Gulf Coast off without giving them a chance just because of your feelings about me. Paradise Point is too important to be held ransom because you and I can't solve our differences. Unless," she added bluntly, "I was right and the committee *is* trying to push Gulf Coast into insolvency so TexAm can move in."

"Do you believe that?"

"No. I think you and your committee were careless and dangerously naive about even talking with TexAm, but I don't believe any of you were being dishonest."

To Kailin's surprise, Brett's strong mouth trembled with a smile. "You don't pull your punches, do you?"

"No." Kailin looked at him evenly. "Brett, I'm very good at my job. I've pulled companies ten times the size of Gulf Coast out of the fire, and there's a good chance I can save Gulf Coast, too. You love this island, and I know you want to do the best for it.... Can't we stop trying to hurt each other long enough to do what's right for Sanibel?"

"Is that what you think we've been trying to do?" he asked quietly. "Hurt each other?"

"Isn't it?" She smiled crookedly, looking down. "I don't know if we're trying to get even or if we're just getting rid of a lot of anger, but I do know it hurts." She glanced up at him. "Funny, I didn't think it would."

"Yeah." His voice was no more than a growl.

Kailin smiled down at the cages, shaking off her sudden pensiveness. The animals were either sleeping peacefully or roughhousing, without a thought to the outside world that had brought them there.

"Six o'clock tomorrow morning."

"What?" Startled, Kailin looked up to find Brett staring down thoughtfully at her.

"I'll pick you up at your apartment at six tomorrow morning. We'll go in by canoe, through the mangroves and marsh to the east. It'll bring us in on the far side, well back of the road."

"You realize that if we get caught in there we can be charged with trespassing."

Brett suddenly grinned the reckless rebel's grin she recognized and loved so well. "Your old man tried often enough and it never stuck. Figure Bryant will have any better luck?"

Kailin laughed. "My father swore he'd see you hanged on that front gate—and police chief Feniak right along side of you. He was sure you and Feniak had a deal going. Dad would have you arrested and you'd be out an hour later, charges dropped on one technicality or another." She smiled, reminiscing, then drew in a deep breath. "But I didn't come here just to ask you to get me into Paradise Point," she said quietly. "I...thought I should tell you about Becky. And about the baby. Your...baby."

Nine

Kailin," Brett said softly, "you don't have—"

"Yes," she replied firmly, "I do." She got to her feet and turned to look at him. He was watching her silently, his eyes filled with a thousand questions she knew he would never ask. "For years I blamed myself. The doctors all said that wasn't the case, but I couldn't get over the feeling that perhaps if I'd been more careful, if...oh, I don't know. A thousand different things." She wandered along the row of cages restlessly. "I think of all the things that happened during those weeks, losing the baby was the worst." She swallowed, remembering the aching loss, the loneliness. "Everyone was so matter-of-fact about it," she whispered. "The doctors, my parents. They said no damage had been done and that I'd be able to have other children." She shivered slightly, rubbing her arms. "No damage! I'd lost the most precious thing in the world to me, and they said there'd been no damage!"

Brett was silent and Kailin kept her face turned resolutely away, knowing that if she looked at him she'd burst into tears. "I wanted that baby so much," she whispered. "It was all I had left of you. As long as I had it, there was hope—that you'd come back, that we still had a chance. But when I lost the baby, there was just . . . nothing."

"Kailin . . ." Strong hands cupped her shoulders, turned her against his chest. "If I'd only known! I could have—"

"Could have what?" Kailin asked him gently, glancing up at him. "I was married, remember?" She laughed quietly and rested her cheek on his chest, relaxing into the warmth and comfort of his arms. "Poor Royce. It was probably the worst honeymoon in history— I spent the first two days crying over losing you, then a week later I had the miscarriage and scared the daylights out of everybody."

Brett murmured something and tightened his arms comfortingly around her.

"Oh, Brett," she whispered, trying not to cry. "Can you ever forgive me?"

"There's nothing to forgive," he said softly. "Kailin, it wasn't your fault."

They stood, holding each other, talking about the eleven years between them, what the two of them had done and thought and felt. It was a healing time, a time of sharing. They were silent for a long time, and finally Kailin laughed, pushing away the past. "Six tomorrow morning, you said?"

Brett blinked, as though just coming back from some distant place. "I—yeah." He shook his head as though scattering a few memories of his own. "Six sharp. Wear jeans and a long-sleeved shirt, good walking shoes, socks, the works—the mosquitoes and no-see-ums are going to be as thick as dogs at a tree growers convention."

"Just what, exactly," Kailin asked in a preoccupied manner, "*are* no-see-ums?"

"What you're looking for and can't find." The paddle sliced the still, obsidian surface of the water without a ripple, and Brett leaned into the stroke.

Kailin was sitting in the bow of the canoe, facing him, looking annoyed as she peeled down her sock to scratch furiously at her ankle. "How do they get through my clothes?" she asked indignantly.

"They can get through just about anything. There's a bottle of repellent in the top pocket of my pack. And don't scratch those bites—it'll only irritate them."

Kailin's look was eloquent, but when she opened the bottle she held it at arm's length and wrinkled her nose. "You can't be serious!"

"Eau de swamp," Brett teased. "Either you put it on and spend the rest of this expedition in relative comfort or get finicky and suffer."

"This stuff is really repulsive," Kailin muttered, but slathered it on everywhere.

"The bugs think so, which is the whole point."

"Look at that! I think it's working already!" She grinned at Brett. "Thank you, Tarzan." She started looking around her with interest, no longer distracted by the clouds of mosquitoes and gnats that in places were so thick that they looked like smoke.

It was still early enough in the morning that the swamp was shrouded with tattered sheets of mist. Clumps of mangroves rose eerily around them, mysterious in the gray half-light. They were more an interwoven knot of branches than individual trees, the tangled, curving roots creating a maze so thick that nothing but the smallest swamp creature could navigate them. Now and again they could make out the crisp white outlines of ibis as they stood like carved ivory statues in the trees, ghostly in the mist.

It was very still and quiet. Occasionally the stillness was shattered as a heron exploded upward in a flurry of wing-beats, then the silence would fold around them again, as tangible as the mist drafting across the black mirrored surface of the water.

"It's beautiful in here, isn't it?" Kailin whispered, staring out at the mangroves in fascination. The sun was starting to burn off the mist and the swamp seemed to take fire, aglow in a ruby haze. Suddenly wave after wave of ibis swirled overhead, followed by low-flying flocks of roseate spoonbills in their blushing plumage. In the distance, like some primordial heartbeat, came the deep, solitary groan of a bull gator.

"It's hard to believe that places like this still exist. It's as though time has gone by without even touching it."

"Oh, it's touched it." Brett dug the paddle into the glassy water, pivoting the bow to avoid a snag as he maneuvered them deftly through the maze of hummocks and tiny islands. "Look more closely and you can see garbage washed up among the mangrove roots, and that's the least of the problems. There's—oh hell!" He laughed good-naturedly. "Don't get me started!"

"Is this the land TexAm promised to turn over to you?"

"Part of it." He swung the canoe gracefully into a passage between two silent, mist-cloaked islands. "We're coming up to Paradise Point now. Look to your right."

Kailin turned her head, and sucked in her breath as they glided out into open water. The sickle shaped curve of sand in the small bay glowed like liquid gold, and in the morning light the long, low point of land looked every inch like paradise.

Brett sent the canoe sweeping into the clear, still water of the tiny bay. "Phase Two is just there—" He pointed north. "Or what's left of it. They built a road down to the bay, but it hasn't been paved yet."

"And Phase Three?"

"The marina's to be just around that spit of land, and they plan to build the helipad out that way." He swung his arm eastward, encompassing open water dotted with small islands. "They're going to fill all that in."

"Fill it in?" Kailin echoed. "You mean join all those little islands together?"

"That's right."

Kailin looked thoughtful. "What happens if a storm hits? Can they anchor the helipad firmly enough to keep it from being washed away?"

"No one will know that until it happens."

Kailin looked at him sharply. "Cut the tour-guide routine, Brett. What's *your* opinion?"

"If they drive pylons through the mud and get down to bedrock, they might be able to hold it together. But as far as I've seen the swamps are designed to take the changing wave action; any rigid man-made structure isn't."

"The helipad and road would run across the direction of the waves and wind instead of with them. They'll take the full force of both," Kailin said, almost to herself.

Brett was surprised to feel a surge of respect at Kailin's immediate grasp of the situation. He found himself wondering what untested strengths lay hidden under her cool and self-possessed exterior. And just how did this new Kailin McGuire fit into his life—if, indeed, she fit there at all?

He beached the canoe on the sand and pulled it well up onto dry land, tucking it under the low-hanging branches of a sea grape tree. Kailin strode up the shelving beach to the grassy meadow above it, and Brett following, enjoyed the tantalizing view she presented. Her soft, faded blue jeans hugged her like a lover's caress. Her waist seemed to disappear while her legs went on forever, and he grinned as he watched her with frank appreciation. He was happy to treat her as an equal in their business dealings, he reminded himself virtuously, but at times like this a man could be forgiven a moment or two of lustful admiration.

She stopped at the top of the slope and looked down at him sharply, as though suddenly aware of the show she was providing. He wiped the grin off his mouth and pretended to be deeply engrossed in something on the horizon. Lustful admiration was one thing; getting caught at it quite another.

"There's a dirt track back here that will lead us into Phase Two," he said innocently, nodding toward the right. "It's about half a mile."

"Half a mile!" She looked up at him. "The Phase Two condos are advertised as being right on the water."

"They are." He smiled, a bit maliciously. "And after the storm last week, some of them are right *in* the water." He took her elbow and guided her down the muddy road. "The area around the bay where we landed is reserved for the luxury condos in Phase Three. Phase One is midrange. It's good, solid housing, nothing too pretentious, but obviously a quality setup. Bryant used them as the lure to sign people up for Phase Two."

"Then built Phase Two sub-standard, according to you."

"You'll see for yourself," he told her calmly. "Watch your footing...."

Kailin sank ankle-deep into mud and water, and she grabbed Brett's hand. "Lovely country," she said dryly, then asked, "What happens to all this wildlife when this complex is finished?"

"Some of it will die," Brett said with brutal honesty. "A lot of good nesting and foraging area will be lost when the helipad and the golf course go in. The birds will probably move down island, but the turtles will have a bad time. The gators, too. They're territorial: as the wilderness area gets smaller they don't take kindly to being crowded closer together. Diminished food supplies lead to scavenging, and that creates a whole new set of problems, but all this is in my report."

"I know. But it's different seeing it." A blue heron sailed by only feet over their heads, and Kailin looked up as the shadow crossed her face, smiling as she watched it flap lazily away.

Why couldn't all their days together be as pleasant as this one? she wondered. There hadn't been a harsh word passed between them since he'd picked her up this morning. Maybe the healing had finally started. Perhaps all the shouting had purged the rest of Brett's anger and they could both put the past behind them.

Brett stopped. They were at the top of a low rise, and as Kailin gazed down at a marshy meadow where a circle of concrete foundations rose from the mud and water like the ruins of some ancient pagan monument. Some of the foundations held the skeletons of buildings, and lumber and brick lay strewn around in untidy piles.

"Welcome to Paradise Point," Brett said quietly.

"But..." Kailin stared down in dismay. "But there's nothing here!"

Brett simply smiled and started down the incline.

"This...this isn't possible," she whispered, gazing at the twisted piles of plywood sheeting. She realized she was looking at what was supposed to be the small four-unit complexes facing the bay. She let her gaze follow the curving line of bare foundations to where they disappeared underwater. "There's got to be some mistake, Brett. No storm could do this!" Suddenly chilled, she strode over to what looked like bulldozed rubble. Slowly, as she stared, it started to take faint but recognizable form. She swallowed, her mind spinning.

"This...is supposed to be the main lodge," she whispered. "There's a pool under there somewhere. Saunas, an exercise club." Numbed, she turned to look at the rest of the complex. "It looks as though it just...exploded."

"It did," Brett said. "That storm hit this place and blew it apart. If it had happened with full occupancy it would have been a slaughter. Most of the people buying these units are seniors—what chance would they have had? They built the access road right along the bay. It was underwater before the storm even hit its peak, cutting off the only escape—and the only access for emergency vehicles. Anyone here would have been trapped.''

Kailin drew in a deep, unsteady breath, pulled her small notebook from her canvas shoulder bag and rummaged around for her camera. She handed it and a handful of film to Brett. ''I want photos—every angle. I want shots of the layout, the nonexistent beach, the road. I want—'' She stopped, narrowed eyes scanning the scene around them. ''I want enough to take to an investigations hearing, because I'm going to blow this thing wide-open.''

She looked up at Brett angrily. ''This couldn't have happened unless someone was paying off the inspectors. They check each stage of construction, and they're not *this* blind. Someone got to them.''

''What happens now?''

''I take all this back to Charlie Bryant who—if he knows what's good for him, and he does—will notify the authorities. Heads will roll in Gulf Coast, and when the dust settles I suspect our good friend Craig Bryant won't be around. A new proposal for Phase Two and Three will be assembled. *If* I can convince the bank to carry the loans for another year, and *if* I can convince your committee that Gulf Coast, under new management, is to be trusted, maybe we'll salvage this mess.'' She smiled suddenly, feeling the familiar surge of adrenaline that she thrived on.

''You love this, don't you?''

Kailin looked up at him in surprise, then laughed. ''Does it show?''

''You're giving off enough energy to light up Miami.''

Still grinning, Kailin nodded. ''Yeah, I love it. I love the wheeling and dealing, the trade-offs. It's like a gigantic game of strategy, and when I finally bring both sides in a dispute like this together, I feel like I've won a war.''

Brett stared down at her, his eyes quizzical, almost pensive. Then he nodded and flipped the lens cap off. ''Okay, where do you want to start?''

Ten

_____

It was nearly noon by the time they finished. Kailin snapped her notebook closed in relief and stretched luxuriously, working the knots out of her back and shoulders. "I've never been so hungry in my life," she groaned.

"There are probably a few edible roots around here I could dig up, if you like."

"Roots, nothing," she muttered. "I want steak and potatoes."

"How about pâté, Brie, sliced turkey breast, artichoke heart salad, fruit, wine...?"

"Don't be cruel, Douglass. It's a long way home."

"Maybe we don't have to go that far."

Kailin's eyes narrowed. "You're up to something. You brought lunch, didn't you?" Kailin grasped the front of his shirt. "You sneak, you packed a lunch and didn't even tell me! That's what's in that rucksack you hauled along."

Brett grinned down at her, slipping his arms lightly around the small of her back. "Oh, I may have a dry crust or two...."

"I think I'm in love!" Kailin clasped two fistfuls of his thick, wind-tangled hair and pulled his face down to hers. "Some days you're too good to be true, Brett Douglass. Thank you, thank you!" She kissed him lightly on the mouth, then started to step away.

His arms tightened instantly, trapping her. His eyes were so deeply blue they rivaled the tropical sky above them. "I just saved your life, and that's the best you can do?" he murmured.

Kailin smiled slowly. "How do I know this isn't an elaborate scam to get me to kiss you?"

"You don't." His warm breath mingled with hers as he brushed his lips across hers. "You'll just have to trust me."

"My daddy always told me never to trust a man who holds all the aces." Kailin caressed his lower lip lightly with the tip of her tongue as she looked up at him. "But then again, what's life without a bit of risk?"

"No life at all," he murmured agreeably, lowering his mouth to hers. Her lips parted almost of their own will.

Kailin felt a shiver run lazily through her when he finally kissed her and she sighed with satisfaction. Yes, she murmured to herself dizzily, some things were definitely worth the risk.

It was a playful, tender kiss that turned, halfway through, into something else altogether. Kailin could feel the change in Brett at the same instant, could sense the tension in every muscle. The kiss became deeper, slower, the play of his tongue turning to a rhythmic thrust that sent a honeyed warmth spilling through her. Her breath caught as every inch of her seemed suddenly brushed with a static charge, and she knew if he ran his hands over her she would give off sparks. Every part of her responded to the unspoken knowledge in that kiss, every secret, hidden place that knew his touch came awake. She heard someone moan softly and let herself melt against him, felt the hard, responding thrust of his body, the urgency in his hands.

She let her head fall back and murmured in pleasure as Brett assaulted her throat. He cupped her head and lifted it so that her mouth was under his again, and he kissed her with an abandoned hunger that fanned the sparks of want to the full-fledged fires of need.

Brett growled something and splayed his fingers around the taut curve of her bottom. He lifted her hard against him, his physical arousal aggressively, conspicuously male. She pressed against him, every nerve ending in her being crying out for the release that his body was promising, and she moaned his name in soft assent.

His responding moan was torn from him, rough and breathless, and he buried his face in the curve of her throat. Kailin could feel him tremble as though fighting a tension that was near explosion, and she clung to him with the same desperate urgency.

Slowly he eased his grip and she slid down his body until she was standing on solid ground, her legs so weak they would never have held her if he'd let go. He hugged her tightly and Kailin rested her cheek on his chest, eyes closed, letting the thump of his heartbeat vibrate through her. Then he eased his arms from around her and Kailin stepped away unsteadily.

She dared to glance up at him, and his eyes trapped hers in a wordless look so eloquent it made her catch her breath. Silently he took her hand and started walking back the way they'd come. They walked in silence, still linked on a thousand different levels. It was as though they had already made love, she thought wonderingly.

When they reached the beach it was unspeakably hot. Kailin peeled off her filthy sneakers and socks and danced inelegantly across the burning sand to the water. She splashed out into the shallow bay up to her knees and stood there in bliss.

"You," Brett said quietly behind her, "are going to get burned to a crisp."

Kailin turned and smiled at him. He'd rolled up his own jeans past his knees and was happily swishing his feet through the water. He lured her over with a tiny triangular cracker mounded with pâté and then gallantly carried her across the hot sand to the tiny tree-shaded clearing where he'd set out the picnic.

He deposited her on the blanket, and Kailin looked around her in astonishment. "Did all this come out of *that*?" She gestured at the rucksack that he'd tossed into the bottom of the canoe that morning. "You *are* a genius!"

How he'd done it, Kailin had no idea, but the end result was magnificent. He'd covered the rough camping blanket with a blue-and-white gingham tablecloth, and in the center had set out a feast worthy of a five-star restaurant. "You always *did* have a fantastic flair for putting together picnics."

"And we usually got rained out," he reminded her, his eyes catching hers, smoky with memories.

She let her gaze slide from his, filled with a warm lassitude. It wasn't just the heat of the day, she knew. It was the nearness of him, the promise she'd read so unmistakably in his look.

Kailin helped herself to a bit of everything, exclaiming with delight as she tried each dish. They ate leisurely, feeding each other crackers and pâté and sipping wine. The silence surrounding them was absolute in the heat of midday, as though even the cicadas were too somnolent to sing. Sheltered in the tiny meadow, surrounded by lacy-leafed trees and bathed by a light, cooling breeze wafting in from the bay, they could easily have been on their own tropical island, isolated from the rest of the world.

Kailin sighed with contentment and Brett stretched, then pulled off his shirt and unsnapped his jeans. He lay back with a sigh, arms crossed under his head, eyes closed.

Kailin tried very hard not to look at him, but found it impossible. He was deeply tanned, with the flat, hard muscle of someone used to physical labor. She looked at him for a long, admiring while, watching the regular rise and fall of his chest. It was only when she let her gaze meander up to his face that she realized he was watching her through half-closed eyes.

The lassitude flowed through her again, thick as melted butter, and she let her eyes slide closed. She didn't move when she heard Brett stir. Even though she'd expected it, Kailin started slightly at the first touch of his mouth. He ran his wine-cool lips across the back of her neck, just above the collar of her blouse, then brushed the side of her neck to the down-soft hollow under her ear with tiny, feathery kisses.

Kailin's toes curled as he pressed his lips into the curve under her lobe. It was more bite than kiss, his teeth grazing her as he sucked gently on her warm, damp skin. Kailin arched her neck slightly, and Brett nuzzled her shoulder and ran his hands down her arms to braid his fingers with hers. She leaned back against him, eyes still closed, feeling herself starting to slowly slip away from reality.

The tension that had started with that kiss over an hour ago had been between them ever since, and she had known it was only a matter of time before he came to her. There was no use fighting it. No use at all . . .

As though sensing the answer she'd given to a question he'd never asked, Brett started leisurely unbuttoning her blouse. As it fell open, he trailed his fingertips down her skin, then tugged the shirt out of her jeans and drew it off. He started kissing her shoulders, and brushed the straps of her bra down. The lacy fabric was delicately peeled back and tossed aside, then he touched her breasts lightly with his flattened palms.

Kailin sighed at the delicious friction and her nipples, already swelling, blossomed fully at his touch. He cupped her breasts, then ran his palms down across her stomach and drew the zipper of her jeans slowly down.

"Take them off," he murmured against her ear.

As though in a dream, Kailin eased her jeans over her hips, then kicked them off. A breeze licked around her legs, sensuously cool as she stretched out.

"Everything." Brett's voice was no more than a husky whisper. "Take everything off, Kailin. I want you naked for me."

Slowly Kailin slipped off her lacy panties. When she'd tossed them aside as well, she relaxed back against Brett. He ran his hands down her stomach slowly, then to her knees and back again, his thumbs trailing fire along her inner thighs. Gently he slid his hands between her legs. Kailin moaned sharply, and Brett whispered something, pausing to nuzzle and kiss the side of her throat.

"Brett..." Kailin arched her back slightly and let her head fall back onto his shoulder, moving restlessly, grasping his arms. "Please, Brett," she breathed, moving her hips toward his teasing hands.

"Not yet," he murmured. "We've got all afternoon."

"Brett!" It was no more than a murmur of regret as he eased himself away from her.

Kailin took a deep unsteady breath and opened her eyes as Brett helped himself to a pineapple spear. He held it up and caught the juice with his tongue, then nibbled from the end of it and held it up to her mouth. She took a bite, then let her head fall back with a smile as he used it like a paintbrush to draw a trail down her chin, then across the taut line of her throat slowly to one breast, where he paused to circle the nipple before continuing his journey. He brushed it lightly across her stomach, then up the inner flesh of one thigh to her knee, where he finally popped it into his own mouth.

Kailin closed her eyes, hardly daring to breath as Brett started licking the juice, each slow swirl of his tongue like the touch of fire and ice. As he moved up her thigh, Kailin sank back onto the blanket and felt that delicious, aching tension within her pull so tight that she was sure it would break. He kissed her softly just at the juncture of her thighs, moved inward and paused. Then, as delicately as a butterfly, he dipped into the nectar of her.

Kailin felt herself melt and open to his caress. She heard a low groan that she only half realized was her own, and the sliding pressure of his tongue increased, perfectly attuned to the intricacies of her. She called to him as the hurricane he was conjuring up threatened to sweep her away, and he paused at that final, precise instant, letting her sense it, savor it, then gently carried her the final distance into heaven itself.

There was a moment of stopped time, a heartbeat during which everything ceased to exist for Kailin but a starburst of pleasure so intense it made her cry out. She opened her eyes and found him watching her, knew by the expression on his face that the pleasure he got from loving her was almost as great as hers.

She raised her arms above her head and stretched, arching her back lightly, luxuriating in the tingling little aftershocks of pleasure. Her body felt so sensitive that even the touch of the breeze sent little tremors through her.

"Witch," he breathed, easing himself down beside her. "I'm burning up...." His teeth grazed her swollen nipples and Kailin murmured in pleasure, her body catching fire again. She moved against him sensuously, his jeans an erotic barrier between her and the arousal she sought, and she sank her fingers into his hair and raised his mouth to hers. His lips parted greedily and then he was kissing her with a fierce, demanding hunger, easing himself over her and pressing her into the springy mattress of grass beneath the blanket.

"You're driving me crazy," she moaned against his mouth. "Take your jeans off!"

"Do you want me, Kailin?" he whispered coaxingly, sliding one denimed thigh between hers.

"Yes!" It was no more than a sob. "I need you, Brett. I need you now...."

"How much?" he growled. "Show me how much, Kailin."

Panting slightly, she gazed up at him through half-closed eyes and guided his hand until his fingers sank into the buttery heat of her.

He needed no further encouragement, and she had to bite her lip to keep from crying out as he moved slowly, drawing sensations from her she couldn't have believed were possible. "You're like honey," he groaned. "Melting and warm and soft as silk..." His fingers moved deeper, and Kailin moaned softly. "Open for me, Kailin," he whispered huskily. "Oh, baby, just relax and let me take you there again. Feel me, Kailin. Feel me there...."

His voice went on and on, coaxing her into responses beyond anything she'd felt before, and she heard herself crying out again and again in pleasure, lost to the wildfire he'd ignited. She didn't even realize that he'd slipped out of his jeans and briefs until he eased himself between her thighs, naked and so ready for her that she gave a tiny gasp of alarm that made him chuckle.

"We've never had a problem before," he murmured reassuringly, and with a thrust of his hips proved with heart-stopping satisfaction that they weren't going to have a problem this time, either.

Kailin clung to him in wonder, knowing with utter certainty that it couldn't get any better. Except that it did: so much better, in fact, that she was soon moving helplessly under him, crying his name over and over again as each long, strong thrust of his body brought her nearer the edge. He was there with her this time, his breath as hot as flame against her throat as he transported them both, and when Kailin finally arched against him with an indrawn sob, tasting the hot salt of her own tears in her throat, she felt her very soul touch his.

Shaken and crying for no earthly reason she could understand, she clung to him through the slow descent, her face buried against his shoulder. It was much later that she felt him stir. He kissed the top of her head and rolled onto his side, cradling her intimately against him, rubbing her back in relaxing circles until she stopped sobbing.

"You all right?" he finally whispered.

She nodded, sniffling, and managed a sob of laughter. "I'm sorry. I—I don't know what happened. It's just that it—it's never been like this before."

Brett slipped his fingers under her chin and tipped her face up, his gaze searching hers. "Like what, Kailin?"

"Just for a moment it was as though I wasn't even me at all, as though I'd become part of you, or you'd become part of me or . . . or something." She swallowed tears.

"That's what love feels like, Kailin. It's what we talked about all those years ago but never really had." He gazed down at her, his eyes filled with such tenderness that it made her heart do a slow cartwheel. "It's what you've never let yourself feel before, Kailin. You've always been so cautious, always holding that little bit of yourself in reserve." He smiled, kissing her gently. "Now it's the real thing, baby."

"Oh, Brett," she gulped, "I *do* love you!"

"I know," he said simply, and the unconditional belief in that simple statement brought tears to her eyes again. "But I didn't mean to make you cry."

"Is there any of th-that wine left?"

Brett picked the bottle up and tipped it assessingly. "Enough for a couple of glasses. Do you want to propose a toast?"

"N-no," Kailin said with a laugh, sitting up and dabbing at her nose with a stray napkin. "I—I've got the hic-hiccups."

"I sunburned my nose," Kailin muttered, peering at her-self in the side mirror of Brett's pickup.

"That's not all you sunburned." Brett grinned, patting her on the bottom as he urged her into the truck. "You're going to have a fine pair of rosy cheeks back here, too, sweetheart. The next time you go skinny-dipping, pick a cloudy day."

"It wasn't *my* idea to go skinny-dipping," she reminded him. She scooted across to the passenger side, pausing to give a despairing glance in the rearview mirror. Sun-bleached and wet, her hair hung to her shoulders in a cloud of sticky tangles. "What a mess! Charlie Bryant and two of his top people are flying in this afternoon to discuss pro-gress. They're going to take one look and *know* I've been rolling around on a deserted beach with the chairman of the Land Use Committee!"

Brett's easy laughter filled the truck. He started the motor and, after checking that the canoe was secure behind, pulled out onto the dirt trail that led to the highway. "What are you going to tell him about this afternoon?" he asked idly. "Craig'll probably have you charged with trespassing if he finds out you've been to Paradise Point."

"He can try," Kailin said with defiance. "But when Charlie Bryant sees these pictures, Craig is not going to have a lot of credibility—especially when he sees the chainsaw marks on those trees barring the access road—the ones that supposedly blew down."

Kailin shook her head slowly, her expression troubled. "Charlie's going to have a fit, Brett. It isn't just his com-pany that Craig's damaged, it's his reputation. He might have forgiven the first, but I doubt he'll ever forgive the second."

"Is he coming out of retirement permanently?"

"I doubt it. I'm hoping to convince him to come back long enough to see the Paradise Point project to completion, but he likes retirement. He says he wants to fish all day, not fight the Brett Douglasses of the world every time he wants to put up a tool shed." She glanced at Brett. "His words, not mine."

"Off the record, Ms. Mediator," Brett said quietly, watching the road, "if you can persuade Charlie Bryant to come out of retirement for this, I can almost guarantee I can convince the committee to okay Phase Three." He looked at her. "But we'll need guarantees, too."

"Such as?"

"Some sort of bond, for one thing. I don't want to approve Phase Three, then have the bank pull the plug on Gulf Coast halfway through. Either the investors stick with Gulf Coast right to the end or they get out right now."

Kailin nodded slowly, eyes narrowed on the road. "It'll take a lot of convincing—banks are pretty skittish when it comes to their own money these days. *They're* going to demand all sorts of guarantees, too."

"Can you do it?"

She turned to give him a challenging look. "Sure."

"Home, or my place first for a shower and...whatever?"

"Whatever?" Her mouth curved up in a mischievous smile. "I'd have thought we'd *whatevered* ourselves out by now."

"Not even close," Brett assured her with a reckless grin, mildly surprised to discover it was true.

By rights, it should take him a week to recuperate from this afternoon, yet just looking at her made his body stir. Without a speck of makeup, her nose sunburned, her hair damp and stringy, she was still so damned beautiful it made his breath catch. Her smile was small and self-satisfied, and he laughed quietly.

"I wish I could, but I have to get home," she said quietly, "I was gone this morning before Becky was even up. She had a pretty busy day lined up for herself, but she was expecting me an hour ago and she frets like a little old woman if I'm late." She smiled fondly. "She was barely three when Royce was killed, but it really shakes a child up to lose a parent suddenly. It was a long time before she could let me out of her sight comfortably. She's over it now—in fact, sometimes I feel she's a little too self-reliant—but underneath I think there's still the suspicion that I might go away one day and never come back, like her father did."

"You two seem to have quite an understanding." Brett looked at her.

"We try. I swore when she was born that I wasn't going to have the kind of relationship with her that I had with my mother, which was no relationship at all. My mother was someone who was either going to or coming from some function. At times it was as though she didn't live there at all but just passed through a lot." She smiled faintly. "You ought to see her with Becky. For that matter, you should see Dad with her—you'd think he'd invented grandparenting."

"Making up for lost time?"

Kailin's smile faded. "I guess so." Brett heard the tightness in her voice and looked at her, but she was staring out the truck window. "He's so sweet with Becky that sometimes I want to scream. I know it's childish, but I find myself wishing he'd treat me that way now and again. I'm his daughter, after all...." She let the words wander off into silence.

"Fathers always demand a lot of their own children," Brett reminded her quietly.

"Maybe. But it wouldn't kill him to say something nice once in a while, would it?" Then she laughed quietly and shook her head. "You'd think I'd be used to it by now, wouldn't you? And the truth is that I'm glad they all get along so well. Becky spends an equal amount of time between my parents and Royce's, and they all seem to benefit."

"You're quite a woman, Kailin McGuire," he said softly, reaching over to slip his hand around hers. "Royce was a lucky man to have had you for those five years."

Kailin's smile turned pensive, and she looked down at their braided hands. "He was a good husband to me, Brett. Better, in a lot of ways, than I deserved."

Brett knew he had to ask the next question, and he hated himself for it. "Did you love him?" His voice was tight, and he stared out at the road, not daring to look at her.

Eleven

Kailin was silent for so long that when he finally did glance at her, Brett found her staring out the side window as though fascinated by the vista of mangrove and palm. "Near the end, I think I did. Not the way I love you, but..." She turned her head to look at him.

He nodded, feeling curiously relieved. He'd wanted her to deny ever having loved Royce, but for some reason finding they'd respected and cared for each other didn't hurt as much as he'd expected. He gave her fingers a squeeze and Kailin curled up against him with a little sigh of happiness.

When they arrived at Kailin's rental complex Becky came racing into the kitchen, shirttails flying, calling out, "Hi, Mom! Boy, am I glad you're home!"

"Hi, honey. Sorry I'm late." Kailin gave her daughter a hug and kicked off her mud-caked shoes. "Am I beat!"

"Good! I mean...you probably won't feel like taking me to the movie tonight, right? Peggy and her mom asked me to go on a sundown beach walk with them, but I told them

I'd sort of promised you that I'd go to a movie." She gazed hopefully at Kailin.

"A sundown beach walk?"

"Ken Ludowski from the parks department puts them on," Brett said. "He gives a talk on tidal ecology and shoreline wildlife, bird and shell conservation, that sort of thing."

"Yeah," Becky put in excitedly. "And afterward they light a bonfire and roast hot dogs and marshmallows and stuff, and—" She sobered. "That is, if you didn't want to go to the movie."

Kailin laughed and gave Becky a fierce hug. "If you want the truth, I'd really rather just stay home."

"Really?" Becky had a hard time containing her delight.

Brett sauntered toward the door. "If you need a ride I can drive you over while your mother has a shower." He grinned at Kailin over Becky's head. "Then I'll come back and keep her company until you get home."

"Great!" Becky's eyes sparkled with mischief as she looked around at Kailin. "There's a couple of real mushy love stories on TV tonight."

"Thank you, Rebecca," Kailin told her with a good-natured smile. "Have fun tonight. Call if you're going to be late."

"Or early," said a laughing voice from the doorway and Linda McAllister stepped in. "I had to dash out for milk, and when I saw the truck in the parking lot I thought I'd see if Becky's coming with us tonight."

"With bells on," Kailin assured her as Becky hurtled out the door. "Thanks, Linda. Do you know Brett Douglass, by the way?"

"Not officially," Linda said, taking Brett's proffered hand. "But Becky's filled me in on all the relevant details."

"Oh, Lord," Kailin groaned.

Linda's grin broadened. "When Becky's ready to come home, I'll give you a call first—just so we don't catch you at an inconvenient moment."

"Linda!" Kailin was astonished to feel herself blushing.

Linda started out, then paused in the doorway. "You know, I have a feeling that after all the fresh air and excitement, Becky will be pretty tired. I think she should stay over at my place. I'll bring her back in the morning."

"Linda!"

"You can thank me later," she said with a smile. She was back an instant later, grinning even more broadly. "And that's quite a sunburn you have there, Mrs. McGuire."

"Yeah," Brett added with a chuckle as the door closed. "When you blush like that, you sort of glow all the way down to your—"

"I'm going to take a quick shower," Kailin said swiftly.

Brett chuckled. "Want some help?"

"I said a *quick* shower," she reminded him. "Showering with you always takes at least an hour."

Kailin stepped out of the shower ten minutes later to find Brett stretched out on the bed in nothing but his unzipped jeans and a drowsy, enticing smile. He meshed his fingers behind his head and watched her with lazy enjoyment as she walked across to the closet and traded the big bath towel she'd wrapped around her for her robe.

She deliberately took her time, knowing he was watching her, knowing he was thinking the same things she was. Smiling to herself, Kailin belted the robe loosely and strolled across to the bed, her eyes holding Brett's. They were hooded and smoky, and when he held his hand out silently she let him draw her down beside him.

Tucking one foot under her, she started drying her hair with the towel. "What are you smiling about?"

"You." His voice was husky. "I was just thinking about how things have changed and yet how they haven't changed at all." He drew her hand to his mouth and started kissing her fingertips, one at a time, swirling his tongue around each as he might something sweet. "I remember lying on my bed in Greenlake, waiting for you to come out of the shower. The place was a dump, and yet when you were there with me it could have been the Taj Mahal. And today, lying here waiting for you, I felt the same kind of anticipation. You were every man's dream come true, Kailin. And you were with me. I used to lie awake nights trying to figure out why."

"I loved you."

"And now, Kailin?" He reached out with his other hand and touched her cheek with his fingers.

Kailin gazed down at him, realizing there was only one answer, had been only the one answer right from the start. "I don't think, down deep where it counted, that I ever stopped loving you, Brett," she whispered.

Brett's deep blue eyes were almost black in the dim light, and they burned into hers with a fierce intensity. "Kailin," he murmured, reaching for her. "Kailin, I—"

He was interrupted by the shrill ring of the telephone, and he dropped back against the pillow with a whispered oath. Laughing softly, Kailin tossed the towel aside and bent over him, kissing his chest. "My answering machine will pick it up," she murmured, swirling her tongue around one of his nipples.

As though obeying her, the machine cut in on the second ring. Only half hearing her standard message, Kailin started moving damp little kisses down across the flat, muscle-corded expanse of Brett's abdomen, then started moving even lower. She could hear his breathing change when she folded back the flap of his jeans.

"You said you'd call this afternoon, Kailin."

Her father's voice, raspy and querulous, was so clear that Kailin recoiled as though the old man himself had suddenly appeared in the room behind her. Brett jackknifed to a sitting position and then he, too, realized what had happened and dropped back onto the bed.

"You know I hate these damned machines," her father went on. "I know you're there listening to me. Pick up the phone!"

Kailin's hand was already reaching for the receiver when Brett caught it firmly. She felt his anger, knew it was less at the interruption of their lovemaking than at who had done the interrupting, felt her own anger—and her guilt. Guilt at just *being* here, she realized with irritation, as though her father had walked in on them and had caught her half-naked in Brett's arms.

"Damn it," she breathed, sitting up and pulling her robe tightly closed. She glowered at the answering machine.

There was an impatient silence as her father waited for her—no, she corrected, as he *willed* her—to answer the phone. Then he decided she either wasn't there or simply wasn't going to answer. "I want to know what's going on down there. Your reports are too sketchy—either those save-the-ecology lunatics are going to approve the continuation of Paradise Point or they aren't. Which is it?"

Kailin stiffened. She glanced at Brett, praying he wasn't really listening, and felt her heart sink when his eyes met hers, puzzled and alert. She started to lean forward to switch the machine off, but Brett caught her wrist firmly.

"Leave it."

"Brett—"

"Leave it," he bit out, his voice deceptively soft.

"But—" She sat back, knowing there was nothing she could say. The damage had already been done; anything else her father said now would just be the frosting on an already unpalatable cake. Why now? she asked her father in silent fury. For heaven's sake, why couldn't you just wait for my call, why do you always have to push and push and push?

"I called earlier and Rebecca said you were out canoeing with Douglass," he went on to say. "I sent you down there to pull Gulf Coast's irons out of the fire, not to lollygag around in the sun with that troublemaker. Take a vacation on *your* time, not mine!"

Kailin felt Brett stiffen. His fingers tightened around her wrist convulsively and he stared at her, the puzzled expression in his eyes vanishing under a growing awareness. She swallowed, knowing she'd just have to sit out the storm and hope that he loved her enough to listen, to understand. To forgive.

"And if he chains himself to the gates *this* time, Kailin, don't you stop the trucks, hear me? This is our last chance. Mess it up and the whole company's gone. If you don't think you can handle it on your own, swallow that damned pride of yours and admit it— I'll find someone to go down and give you a hand. And call me!"

The receiver on that distant phone went down with a bang, the sound hanging in the air like an exclamation mark. Kailin stared at a point on the bed midway between Brett's elbow and her knee, barely breathing, waiting for him to say something. It didn't take long.

"Just what the hell," he asked with deceptive ease, "is your old man up to now?"

"He's not up to anything," she replied with an equally deceptive ease.

"No?" Brett's stare was hard. "Out with it, Kailin."

"It...I...oh, hell!" She stopped and ran her fingers through her tangled hair to shove it off her face. "I should have told you this up front, but I—" She stopped again, realizing her reasons for not telling him didn't matter. "Dad's one of the investors behind Paradise Point. He has everything on the line—the business, the house. Everything."

The silence between them was so highly charged it nearly gave off sparks. Brett dropped her wrist and rolled off the bed in one lithe, easy movement, standing to stare down at her. "I should have guessed something like this was going on," he said in a soft, taut voice. "It was just too much of a coincidence, having you turn up out of the blue to work on this. Just too damned . . . easy.''

"What do you mean, easy?'' she whispered, daring to look up at him.

His eyes glowed like a cat's. "Easy. Gulf Coast is on the verge of going belly-up. The only hope to save it is if the Land Use Committee can be persuaded to approve Phase Three—in spite of obvious deficiencies in the project to date. Along comes Kailin McGuire, the woman out of the chairman's past. There's a little sparring, a little flirting— and Douglass falls for the bait and is firmly hooked. The chairman recommends the committee overlooks the problems with the project and approves Phase Three, the bank agrees not to call in its loans, Gulf Coast wins the day—and old man Quentin J. Yarbro comes out of it with his millions intact.''

Kailin stared up at him. "You can't possibly believe any of that,'' she said in astonishment. "I'm recommending a full-scale investigation of the problems on Phase Two, not trying to cover them up. And—''

"Give a little, get a little,'' Brett said with a hard smile. "You wouldn't hesitate sacrificing Craig Bryant as a show of good faith and to convince the Land Use Committee you mean business.''

"I *do* mean business,'' Kailin said with some annoyance.

Brett gave another harsh laugh, his eyes bitter. "And this afternoon? Was that business, too?''

Kailin sucked in her breath, staring at him in shock. "You can't believe that!''

"Kailin,'' he said wearily, "I don't know what the hell to believe where you're concerned. I can't read you at all. I get to the point where I think maybe I've seen the real Kailin, then you pull a number like this and I'm back to square one.'' He stared at her for a silent moment, his face angry and resigned. "I don't even know who you are.''

"Brett, how can you say that after we—''

"Why didn't you tell me about your father's involvement earlier?"

"It's confidential, for one thing," Kailin said quietly. "He got suckered in by the promise of easy money. It happens all the time, Brett. Dad wants to retire, and he figured he could make a killing on the Paradise Point project."

"And you want to protect him."

"I want to protect all of them. He's not the only investor who'll lose his shirt if Gulf Coast goes under."

"But I'll bet he's the only investor who sent his daughter down here to save the day." He stared at her, his mouth a hard, angry line. "And he *did* send you down here, didn't he? He's behind it."

"He isn't behind anything," Kailin said wearily. "There is nothing underhanded or suspicious involved with any of this, Brett. When the bank contacted my father about the situation he suggested they use me to investigate. I wasn't interested *because* Dad was one of the investors, but I said I'd at least look into it. When I found out that you were involved, I turned the job down flat. Then...oh, I don't know." She threw her hands up in defeat and stood up wearily, wandering over to the windows and staring down at the beach. "This is what I do, and I'm good at it. Maybe it was vanity that finally got me. Maybe I just wanted to prove something to my father. Maybe..." She didn't bother finishing it, shaking her head. "Who knows?"

"And your father?" Brett asked silkily. "I don't suppose that crack about not stopping if I get in your way means what it sounds like?"

"Of course not!" Kailin looked around at him angrily. "He doesn't have anything to do with my company *or* how I do my job. That's just Dad, being his usual tactful, helpful self." She looked at him evenly. "He won't admit it, Brett, but he's terrified he's going to lose everything. He *is* the reason I'm down here—but not in the way you think. After I told the bank I wouldn't take the job if it came gold-plated, he called me. It nearly killed him, having to ask me for help. Even then there was no admission of fault, no please or thank you. I wanted to rub his nose in it, but for some reason I couldn't.'' She sighed, knowing he'd never understand. ''Underneath he was still my father. And he needed me.'' She smiled faintly.

''And I suppose that reminder that he sent you down here—that you're working on *his* time—doesn't mean anything, either.''

''No.'' Kailin felt very tired. ''Although, knowing Dad, he's probably convinced himself that that's the truth. It would be easier for him to accept my help if he's convinced himself that *he's* in charge. But it just isn't like that, Brett. You have to believe me.''

''Believe you, Kailin?'' He snatched up his shirt from a nearby chair, then rammed his arms into the sleeves. His eyes held hers, hot and angry. ''I'd have trouble believing you if you told me what day of the week it is.''

''Brett!''

''You're a damned fool if you think you're running the show, Kailin. And an even bigger one if you think you've convinced *me*. He's manipulating you now just like he always has.''

''Brett, that isn't true!''

''Then give it up.''

Kailin stared at him in confusion. ''Give . . . what up?''

''Gulf Coast. Paradise Point.'' His gaze narrowed. ''Drop the whole thing, Kailin. Just let it go.''

She blinked at him. ''Brett, this is my job.''

''To hell with your job,'' he growled. ''Turn it over to someone else—you're not the only person in the world who can sort this out.''

''But . . .'' Kailin simply stared at him. ''Do you mean that you're asking me to make a choice between my work . . . and you?''

"I'm asking you to choose between your father and me. As long as he—and this suspicion—is between us, Kailin, we can't have any kind of a relationship."

"We don't *have* a relationship if you can demand that," she whispered. "Brett, do you have any idea of what you're asking?"

His mouth was hard and stubborn. "I just know that as long as you're being manipulated by your father, we have no future. I can't love a woman I can't trust, Kailin."

If he'd slapped her across the face, Kailin couldn't have been more stunned. "Damn you, Brett Douglass," she said in a furious whisper. "How *dare* you talk about love and trust when you've just tried to blackmail me into turning my back on a group of people I've given my professional word to help. You're right—you can't love someone you don't trust. But it goes deeper than that, Brett. If you love someone, you *do* trust them—it's that simple. You don't ask them for proof. You don't demand that they give up one thing for another."

Brett stared at her for a long, taut moment, then turned and strode toward the door. "I guess that answers my question, Kailin."

"What question? You haven't *asked* me anything, you've just stood there making accusations!"

Brett stopped dead and paused with his hand on the doorknob. Then he turned to look at her, his eyes shadowed and private. "So are you using me?" he demanded bluntly. "Did you come down here hoping to use our relationship to push approval for Phase Three through my committee?"

Kailin felt something twist inside her, twist and splinter and die. "If you don't think you know the answer to that, Brett," she said very softly, "then it doesn't really matter at all, does it?"

An eerie, breath-held silence slid through the room, thick as smoke. Kailin could feel Brett's hot, angry stare burning into her back, but she refused to turn around, refused to allow him the small victory of seeing her cry. Don't go, she urged him silently. Say you love me, say you trust me. . . .

The door closed quietly behind him. A moment later the outer door to the apartment also closed. The bang reverberated through the room like a clap of thunder. Kailin swallowed very carefully, tasting a hot, salty bitterness in her throat. She shut her eyes and clung to the edge of the dressing table until her fingers ached, knowing that if she let go of it she'd also let go of the paper-thin edge of control she was clinging to.

And her father? She forced herself to face Brett's furious accusation: *was* she simply a pawn? It wasn't inconceivable. He'd known about Brett's involvement in Paradise Point, but he hadn't told her, knowing how she would react. Had he also anticipated what would happen if she and Brett were thrown together?

She felt caught in the crossfire between past and present, between the woman she was and the child she'd been. Between Brett and her father. Always between the two men most important in her life.

Damn it! She picked up the small table lamp and flung it against the far wall. Glass exploded like shrapnel and Kailin stared at it, using every ounce of willpower she possessed to keep from bursting into tears. She'd cried enough tears over the past eleven years to last a lifetime, and she would *not* cry now.

Life hurts. The trick is, don't let it show.

But nothing—*nothing*—was supposed to hurt this badly!

"You're wrong, Daddy," she whispered, her voice catching on the tears she no longer tried to stop. "You're wrong! Because if you really care, you can't help but let it show."

Brett stared out across the whitecaps of the Gulf of Mexico, thinking that those troubled, gray waters exactly matched his mood.

There was a storm brewing out there, out beyond the crescent-moon curve of the Keys where the sea ran deep. The air was hot and tense with it, and the sky along the horizon was clotted with clouds the color of an old bruise. Long, low waves pushed toward the shore, dark as lead and curiously heavy. Even the birds seemed affected. A fleet of pelicans bobbed just offshore, rising and falling with the motion of the waves, and the gulls walking the beach seemed stiff and sullen.

He shoved his hands into the pockets of his jeans, then turned and started trudging up the beach again, kicking at a twisted skein of seaweed. As always, Kailin slipped into his mind. Kailin laughing, her head thrown back, her silver-gold hair blowing in the wind, green eyes alight with mischief....

Damn you, Kailin, why are you torturing me like this? What do you want from me?

He rubbed his temples and swore under his breath, no nearer an answer than he'd been when he'd walked out of her apartment two days ago. She was like the mist, there one moment and gone the next, slipping through his fingers just when he thought he had her pinned down.

She'd been like that eleven years ago. Not a day had passed that long, hot summer when he hadn't wondered, at least fleetingly, why she stayed. She had everything—the rich, beautiful girl from the right side of town. And he'd had nothing. Nothing a woman who had everything could possibly want, anyway.

Was that why he'd let her go? he found himself suddenly wondering. Because he'd never really believed she would stay? Had he thought to lessen the pain of losing her by cutting her out of his life first?

And this time?

I loved you, she'd said the other night. *I stayed because I loved you.*

He closed his eyes, swearing softly.

The storm broke later that night, screaming out of the southeast like a banshee. Brett checked the storm shutters and doors, then poured himself a generous glass of brandy and lit a crackling fire in his little-used fireplace. Smiling at his own self-indulgence, he sank into his favorite chair with a mystery. But he found himself staring unseeingly at the pages, listening to every creak and groan of the house. The wind picked at the shutters like something wanting in, and he finally got to his feet, pacing restlessly.

He stood peering through the storm shutters at the spume flying on the Gulf. The palms along the bottom of his lawn were whipping around like bamboo stalks, fronds shredded, and he watched them with an inner sympathy, knowing exactly how they felt.

How he heard the knock over the noise of the storm, he didn't know. Only half believing anyone would be out in this tumult, he inched the door open. There was something standing out there that looked like a small yellow tent. A wet hand inched out of an oversize sleeve and shoved back the hood of the rain slicker.

Brett stared down at Becky in astonishment. She gazed back miserably, teeth chattering, hair plastered to her head. Saying nothing, he held the door open and she stumbled in, shivering so badly she could hardly walk. She stood unprotesting as Brett pulled the slicker over her head, then ushered her into the living room, pausing on the way to grab a bath towel.

He moved the big square hassock in front of the crackling fire with his foot and pointed to it. Becky sat down, not meeting his eyes, her shoulders hunched, then loosened the drawstring on her sweatshirt and pulled Maverick out. The kitten, rumpled and slightly damp, sneezed, obviously un-amused by whatever was going on.

Brett handed Becky the towel, then sat on the hearth and picked the kitten up, stroking it. "Where's your mother?"

"Home." The voice was muffled as Becky scrubbed her hair with the towel. "I ran away."

He should have been surprised, but he wasn't. Somehow he'd known exactly what had happened from the instant he'd seen her standing out there tonight. "Terrific," he breathed, rubbing the tightness between his eyes. Then he took a deep breath and looked at her. "How did you get up here?"

"I caught a ride with Mrs. Peabody, the librarian."

Now what? he asked himself wearily. Runaway nine-year-olds weren't exactly his area of expertise. He set Maverick in Becky's lap, then got to his feet. "I'll have to call your mother."

"I'm not going back." She looked up at him with the same stubborn set to her mouth, the same glint of steely determination in her eyes, that he'd seen on Kailin's face more times than he cared to remember. "I *won't* go back."

"Becky—"

"I mean it!" She tossed her head indignantly. "I'm going to stay down here with you. You . . . you can adopt me or something!"

He opened his mouth to argue with her, then realized he'd have no more luck arguing with her than he'd ever had arguing with Kailin. She'd obviously inherited more than just blond hair and green eyes from her mother. "You two hungry?" Becky glanced up at him suspiciously, then nodded. Brett sighed and made his way to the kitchen.

He'd started dialing Kailin's number before he realized that the line was dead, and he muttered something impolite under his breath and slammed the receiver down. The electricity was the next to go. It plunged him into darkness at the precise instant he was pouring cocoa into a mug, and he said something even more impolite as he slopped the scalding-hot liquid over his hands. The generator kicked in a moment or two later, and the low-voltage lights he'd installed at strategic corners flickered on, banishing the sudden, utter darkness.

Sucking the back of his hand, he carried the mug of cocoa and a dish of warm milk into the living room. Becky smiled a tentative thank-you and placed the dish in front of Maverick, who promptly curled his tail around his feet and shoved his face into the milk, lapping greedily. Becky cradled the mug in her hands and sipped the cocoa, and Brett dug out the candles and lighted them.

He picked up his glass of brandy and sat on the hearth again, watching the kitten eat. "I tried calling your mother, but the lines are down."

"That's okay," Becky muttered.

"Interested in talking about it?"

Becky ran her finger along the rim of the mug, then sighed deeply. "We had a fight. She wants to go back to Indiana tomorrow, but I don't want to go." She glanced at Brett. "I want to stay down here with you."

"She's leaving tomorrow?" It was out before he could stop himself, an arrowlike shaft of pain.

"She said you guys had a...disagreement." Becky glanced at him again. "But it was worse than a disagreement, wasn't it?"

"Yeah," he breathed, staring into the brandy. "It was worse."

"Do you love her?"

It was like being hit by a truck. Brett lifted his head to stare at her, fighting to catch his breath. Becky gazed back at him through her mother's clear green eyes, free of guile or trickery, and Brett heard himself whisper *yes* before he'd even realized what had happened.

Becky frowned. "Then I don't understand why she wants to leave."

"It's not that simple, Becky," he said with quiet desolation. "Sometimes loving someone just isn't enough."

"That doesn't make any sense," she said flatly.

Brett smiled humorlessly. "No one's ever been able to make sense out of love, Becky. Love just . . . is."

She was silent as she thought it over. "Can I stay here for good?"

"Becky—" He stopped, temporarily defeated. Now what? He had a sudden vivid image of Kailin having him arrested for kidnapping.

"You can probably adopt me," Becky said calmly. "After all, I was supposed to be your daughter." Brett lifted his head to stare at her uncomprehendingly, and she shrugged. "She told me that she was expecting your baby before she got married to my father. But then she lost that one and had me instead." She smiled a glowing smile that seemed to light up the room. "So you see, I was supposed to have been yours. I *feel* like your daughter, if that means anything."

"Oh, Becky," he breathed, aching with a deep, indefinable sadness. How in God's name had he and Kailin become so inextricably entangled that even this child, born more than a year after he'd left Greenlake, was herself caught? It was as though those intervening years had been no more than a heartbeat. How long, he wondered, would it take for them to finally be free of each other?

And suddenly he knew, with a certainty so deep it chilled him, that eleven or even eleven hundred years would never be long enough. They were parts of a whole, linked in some way they would never be able to understand—or ever be able to break.

Becky yawned, and Brett realized with a shock that it was well past midnight. Maverick had fallen asleep with his nose on the edge of the milk dish, and Brett picked him up and tucked him into Becky's sweatshirt. "Come on, you two. Maybe things will make some sense in the morning."

But after he'd gotten child and kitten tucked into the bed in the spare room, Brett found himself too restless to sleep. He prowled the darkened house, checking windows he'd checked twice before, peering out into the storm-lashed night as though something might have changed in the past two minutes. Lightning flickered incessantly, and the thunder mumbled and roared over the distant boom of breakers.

When the car lights flickered through the shutters on the side window, he thought at first it was just lightning. But then he heard the sound of an engine and eased himself to his feet, smiling grimly as he took a bracing swallow of brandy.

Twelve

Kailin tried to keep the hood of her slicker up as she ran to the house, but the wind tore it out of her hands. It didn't matter anyway, she realized numbly as she fought her way through the stinging wind: she was already soaking wet and chilled to the bone. Brett was waiting for her, standing in the open door. He was silhouetted against the soft light, and he looked very large and solid and calm. And in that instant she knew everything was all right.

"She's here," he said without preamble, pulling the slicker over her head and tossing it on a nearby deck chair.

Kailin nodded and walked in, shivering so badly she had to clench her teeth to keep them from rattling. Rainwater ran into her eyes and she smoothed her soaking hair back, staring around the comfortable living room in wonder. A fire crackled in the hearth, and the room was filled with dozens of candles of all colors and shapes, bathing everything with a soft golden glow that seemed to reach out and gather her into its warmth.

"I knew she'd come here," she whispered. "We had a horrendous fight and she grabbed Maverick and stormed out before I could stop her." A shiver made her teeth rattle, and Brett took her by the arm and led her across to the fireplace. He sat her firmly on the hearth and draped a bath towel around her shoulders, then walked away.

Slowly she started rubbing her hair dry, feeling the heat from the fire start to seep through her. "I tried to call you, but the phones are dead. So I decided to drive up. But the road's underwater in places and it took forever just to get to Blind Pass and the waves were breaking right across the highway on the Captiva side. Then I got lost and—" She had to stop, an unexpected sob threatening to escape.

"She's fine, except for being wet and cold and mad as hell. She's asleep in the spare room."

Kailin nodded. There was an empty mug that looked as though it had once held hot chocolate sitting on the hearth beside her, and a small dish half filled with milk. She had to laugh. "I see you were dispensing sympathy and first aid."

"It seems to be my night for it." He handed her a glass. "You look like you could use some yourself. Drink that."

Kailin cupped the glass between both palms to keep from spilling it and took a swallow. The brandy made her eyes water, but its glowing warmth started to spread through her almost instantly. "I'm sorry about all of this. She's too much like her mother at times—acts first and worries about the consequences later." She paused. "And I suppose she thinks she can bring us together. She wants to see me happy, and she thinks you're part of that." Kailin stared at the glass. "Maybe I thought so, too."

"She says you're leaving." He spoke without inflection, sitting in the big armchair across from her, one foot braced on the edge of the hassock, the glass of brandy balanced on his upraised knee. The firelight played across the strong planes of his face, giving it a hardness that she'd never seen before.

Kailin nodded, turning the glass in her hands. "It was a mistake, coming here," she said after a long while. "I kept telling myself that I was down here because I'd committed myself to this job, but of course that was just an excuse. I was down here because of you." She didn't look at him, terrified of what she might see on his face. "I realize now I'd hoped that we'd just pick up where we'd left off. Somehow I thought it would be that easy...."

She let the sentence trail off, not certain of what she was trying to say. "I thought that loving you was enough. I thought that if I had the chance to tell you, everything would be all right." She took a deep breath, wishing the brandy and fire would warm that icy, empty little spot where her heart had been. "But I was wrong. It takes more than just words. It takes trust. And we just don't...seem to have that."

She did look up at him then, a quick glance that told her nothing. He was simply watching her. The silence between them lengthened, broken only by the soft mutter of the flames. Even the storm seemed to have receded, and Kailin listened absently to the distant moan of the wind. She turned the glass in her hands, waiting, waiting....

"And Paradise Point?" he finally said, his voice rough, as though he hadn't used it in week. "Are you leaving it, too?"

For some reason, that nearly made Kailin smile. She realized in that instant that she'd been waiting for him to tell her he loved her, that he *did* trust her, that he couldn't live without her. All the things that he was supposed to say to make it better. But in the end it came back down to one thing: Paradise Point.

"Yes." She was surprised to hear her voice so calm. Surprised, too, that she felt so little pain. Maybe letting go was the answer, she thought curiously. Maybe that was all it took. She looked at the glass for a moment, then set it aside and stood up, looking at Brett calmly. "But not because you

asked me to. I'm leaving because my involvement with the
project is jeopardizing the entire thing.

"It isn't fair to everyone concerned for us to use Paradise Point as ammunition against each other in our private
little war, and since you can't seem to separate the two, I'll
do it myself. I've worked up an interim report and proposal
with the approval of both the bank and Charlie Bryant. It'll
be delivered to you tomorrow, and you can present it to the
committee. If it doesn't fit your requirements, make a
counterproposal and send it to the bank in Miami. They'll
assign another mediator to work with you."

It seemed to take him by surprise. He looked at her, then
frowned and nodded, staring thoughtfully at the glass in his
hand. He drew circles with it on his knee, tipping the brandy
this way and that.

Say something, damn it, she nearly screamed at him.
Then, as quickly as it had erupted through her, the anger
and impatience were gone. In their place was nothing but a
bone-deep weariness, and she got to her feet slowly, nearly
staggering with exhaustion. She'd worked for two straight
days getting that report finished, phone in one hand and a
pen in the other, surrounded by cups of cold coffee and a
daughter whose patience had finally given out tonight.
Whether it had been worth it, time would tell. Right at the
moment, all she wanted was a hot bath and about twelve
hours of sleep.

Brett looked up at her. She thought for a moment that he
was going to say something, then realized it had just been
her own wishful thinking. She smiled wryly. "I'd better
collect my daughter and leave before the storm gets worse."

"Where the hell have you been, boy?" Zac Cheevers
strode into Brett's office with the subtlety of a freight train,
the ever-present dead cigar sticking pugnaciously from one
corner of his mouth.

It was odd, Brett found himself thinking, but he'd never seen Cheevers actually *smoking* one of the damned things. "What can I do for you, Zac?"

Zac blinked at him, then hooked a chair nearer with his foot and settled his bulk into it. "I'd say you've already done it." He tossed a thick wad of papers onto the desk.

"What is it?" Brett stared at the thing without interest.

Zac gazed contemplatively at Brett, chewing on the cigar. "You all right, boy? You look paler than a frog's belly, and about as low. Should give yourself a dose of tonic, get some color back in you."

Brett smiled faintly. "Start practicing medicine Zac, and I'll start handing out free legal advice."

Zac grunted. "After seeing the fancy footwork you pulled on that proposal, I'd say you could do better 'n' some I know."

Brett looked up blankly. "What proposal?"

Zac looked at Brett in exasperation, pointing to the papers he'd thrown on the desk. "What the hell's wrong with you, Douglass? Old Charlie Bryant's been wanting to meet with us since Tuesday, and I've been putting him off until I could find you."

"Sailing," Brett said tiredly, combing his hair back with his fingers. "I went... sailing." Thinking, was what he meant.

"You've just pulled off the coup of the century and you're off sailing." Zac gave an elephantine snort.

It was starting to irritate Brett now, and he almost relished the bite of anger. Any feeling was better than the numbed emptiness he'd been living with. "Zac, I've been out in the middle of nowhere for four days. I have no idea what you're talking about."

Zac glowered at Brett from under beetling, shaggy brows. "I am talking about a proposal put together by your lady friend, *Ms*. McGuire. I don't know how she swung it—I don't know how *you* swung it—but Gulf Coast's fixin' to

give you everything you asked for, with a bit besides—
starting with that wildlife sanctuary."

He leaned forward and set the proposal on the edge of
Brett's desk, his voice holding none of its usual easy drawl.
It was the voice of the shrewd courtroom lawyer he was, and
Brett settled down to listen. "Leaving out all the double-talk
and legalese, it boils down to one thing—if we approve a
revised plan for Phase Three, the bank will agree to float
Gulf Coast's loans for two years, interest suspended for one
of those two, to free up operating capital.

"I'll tell you, Douglass, that little lady of yours knows
how to play the game. Give a little, take a little." He shook
his head in amused admiration.

"Yeah," Brett said quietly. "She does that." Then he
shook off the sudden pensiveness and looked at Zac. "And
Phase Three?"

"Well, they scrapped the golf course and helipad for a
start." Zac ignored Brett's startled look. "They're going to
negotiate a deal with the neighboring resorts for use of their
golf courses and use the island pad and chauffeur the guests
back and forth with limos. Save a fortune."

And the nesting herons, Brett thought to himself, remembering the expression of delight on Kailin's face as
she'd watched the big birds.

"They've cut the total number of units, but the remain-
ing ones will be top-of-the-line luxury. But the best part is
that they're going to turn over that whole back wetlands as
a wildlife conservation area on the provision that they can
offer limited, controlled access for guided nature walks,
canoe trips, birding trips and so on."

Brett stared at the proposal in Zac's hands, a feeling of
unreality stealing over him. "What about Craig Bryant and
the construction problems they're having?" he asked in a
tight voice. There had to be a catch. Damn it, there had to
be!

"The whole thing is contingent on dumping the existing people and using Charlie's people. And last I heard, Craig was headed west. His daddy kicked him out." Brett gave a low whistle, and Zac chuckled. "Next time you see that lady of yours, you tell her she done real good."

"I will," Brett breathed. He was just starting to comprehend the enormity of what Kailin had done.

Zac raised an eyebrow and got to his feet, shoving the cigar to the other side of his mouth. "Hell, boy, if you don't marry that gal, you're a damned fool. And if you do, bring her back and give her a job. I like her style."

Deep in thought, Brett didn't notice Zac's departure. What had Kailin said that last night? *It takes more than just words. It takes trust....* She must have been working day and night to pull this off. She'd known exactly what it would take to make the Paradise Point project possible, and she'd gone out and put it together. A parting gift, perhaps. Her way of saying goodbye.

God, he loved her!

He closed his eyes, a sudden wave of emptiness and utter loss engulfing him. He felt hollow and sick and so filled with bleak despair it was like a tangible ache.

Guilt. He stared at the proposal lying on his desk. You're coming down with a bad case of guilt, my friend. He must have gone a little crazy to think it was a matter of Kailin choosing one thing or another. It didn't have anything to do with Paradise Point or even with her father. It had to do with eleven years of guilt and the knowledge that he'd deserted her when she'd needed him the most. How could he forgive her when he hadn't learned to forgive himself?

He didn't know if he'd said the words aloud or not, but they rang through the silences of his mind like a cry from the heart— "Oh, God, Kailin . . . what have I done?"

It took him nearly three hours. It would have taken a fraction of that had he used some common sense, but it was only after he'd been trying her Indianapolis phone number for two hours and fifty-five minutes that he remembered it was Thanksgiving weekend.

He didn't have to even look the number up, it was still fresh in his mind. It gave him a strange feeling, dialing those numbers after all this time, and he found himself holding his breath as the phone on the other end rang. A woman with a French accent said Kailin was there and went to find her, leaving Brett to listen to the hum of the open line with growing impatience. Then someone picked up that distant receiver, and he smiled in anticipation.

"That you, Douglass?"

The voice was slurred slightly, but Brett had no difficulty recognizing it. The sound slammed him into the past so painfully that it all but knocked the breath out of him. He closed his eyes, his hand aching where he was clutching the receiver.

"I said, is that you, Douglass?"

It was an imperious voice, used to giving orders, used to being obeyed. Brett felt the slow, sour rise of anger, and had to fight the urge to slam the receiver down. "Yes," he said after a moment. "It's me."

There was silence, crackling with distance. "My daughter doesn't want to speak with you, Douglass. And I don't want you talking to her. Don't call here again."

The receiver went down, hard. Again there was a shifting of time as past and present merged like two out-of-focus pictures. He was twenty-six again and full of fire, battling dragons and in love with the most beautiful princess of all.

He wasn't going to let her go.

"Not this time," Brett vowed through gritted teeth as he strode to the door. "You may have run me off once, old man, but this time I'm fighting for her with everything I've got!"

The mansion on River Road was unchanged. Set back in the trees on its three acres of lawns and gardens, it looked out over river and town like a feudal castle, radiating wealth and power. As he drove through the estate gates and up the long, winding drive, Brett felt as though he were traveling back through time.

To his surprise, they let him in.

He'd half expected Yarbro himself to come to the door, had anticipated a showdown and was almost disappointed. He followed the French maid down the corridor, through a tall carved door. She said something in French to a uniformed nurse, whose eyes settled momentarily on Brett, as though sizing him up for possible emergency treatment. Then she and the maid left without a word.

The room was overly warm. A fire sputtered on the hearth, adding what Brett figured was unnecessary heat to the stuffiness. Tall windows looked out over the gardens, and in the distance Brett could see the stables, the tennis courts.

"Well, come over here, damn it. Where I can see you. Quit skulking around in the shadows."

It was only then that Brett realized he wasn't alone. He hadn't seen the old man sitting in the shadows by the hearth, and as he stared across the room at Quentin J. Yarbro, Brett realized that at least here, time hadn't stood still.

He was an old man now. Not frail—Brett couldn't imagine Yarbro ever being frail—but the signs of advancing years and illness were there. He looked smaller than Brett remembered, but perhaps it was just the big chair or the soft lap robe tucked carefully around his legs. He didn't get to his feet as Brett approached, and Brett noticed with a slight shock that there were two walking sticks tucked unobtrusively beside him.

Only the eyes hadn't changed. They were still as hard as agate, and they homed in on Brett's like twin spotlights. "I was wondering if you'd have the guts to come after her this time."

Brett blinked. It was not by any stretch of imagination the greeting he was expecting.

While he was considering his options, the gray head turned toward a nearby doorway. "Roberts!" A tiny white-haired man appeared almost instantly. He carried a tray across to the desk and set it down. Yarbro peered suspiciously at the silver teapot. "What the hell's that?"

"Herbal tea, sir."

"Tea?" The bellow rattled the china cups. "Bring me some coffee. *Real* coffee, not that decaffeinated garbage they've been trying to get me to drink."

"Sir," Robert said with a weary resignation, as though he'd fought this battle many times before, "you know the doctor—"

"Roberts, do you enjoy working here?"

"Yes, sir."

"Then get me some coffee!" Yarbro waited until Roberts had collected the tray and retreated with it before breaking into a sly chuckle. "Good man, Roberts. You just have to shout at him now and again to keep him in line." He eyed Brett assessingly. "Want a drink?"

"Not particularly."

"Well, I do. Get me one—bottom drawer of that cabinet over there. Have to hide the damned stuff or they throw it out." Brett hesitated, torn between sympathy for the man's doctor and a sudden, unexpected sympathy for Yarbro himself. Yarbro glared at him. "Now don't you start! My family's treating me like a damned invalid. A man has a heart attack and you'd think he was incapacitated, for God's sake. One drink isn't going to kill me, Douglass!"

"If I thought there was a possibility," Brett said dryly as he walked across to the cabinet, "I'd have brought you a bottle."

Yarbro gave a snort of laughter. "Well, well, well. Grown up a bit, have we? You'd have told me to go to hell eleven years ago, Douglass." He took the glass of liquor that Brett held out. Something moved in his lap, and Brett was astonished to see Maverick curled up in a fold of the robe. Yarbro started stroking the kitten absently. "So you think you're going to get my daughter this time, do you?"

Brett didn't say anything. He strolled across to the windows and stared out at the winter-brown gardens, wondering where this was leading.

"The only things in this life worth having are the things worth fighting for, Douglass." He took a swallow of the whiskey, smacking his lips with satisfaction.

"I didn't come here to fight with you. Or to rehash the past." Brett turned and looked at the old man steadily. "I'm going to marry your daughter, Yarbro, like it or not."

Expecting an explosion, Brett was surprised when Yarbro simply nodded, staring speculatively at him. "Are you approving Phase Three of the Paradise Point project?"

To his surprise, Brett discovered he could still laugh. "You never give up, do you?" he asked with a shake of his head. "I won't negotiate a bride price with you, Yarbro. You can't barter human lives, trading a bit of this for a bit of that. Paradise Point—and your investment—has got nothing to do with Kailin and me."

Yarbro's sharp, bright eyes narrowed very slightly. "You never did scare easily, Douglass. That was one thing I always admired about you."

"Oh, you got to me, all right," Brett assured him. "It was because of you that I turned my back on the only woman I've ever loved and I've had to live with that guilt for eleven years."

"It takes a lot of courage to admit when you're wrong." Yarbro stared into the glass in his hand, his expression pensive. "There haven't been many men in my life who've stood up to me, Douglass. Maybe that's why I admire your courage so much. And I'm not talking about physical courage, I'm talking about the inside kind—the moral kind."

"Have you ever taken a good look at your own daughter?"

A tiny smile lifted one corner of Yarbro's mouth. "I have."

Brett nodded, looking at the drink he'd poured for himself and hadn't even tasted yet. "I love her," he said quietly.

"So do I."

The admission was spoken so softly that Brett looked up in surprise, scarcely believing he'd even heard it. His eyes met Yarbro's, and in that instant he felt something shift in the room, and the tension was gone. Suddenly they were no longer opponents but simply two men sharing insights and good whiskey on a blustery November afternoon. He smiled and took a sip, feeling the rich, smoky heat curl around his tongue like satin.

Yarbro lifted his glass in what might have been a salute. Then he swallowed the contents and set it aside, that fleeting glimpse of gentleness gone. "Think you're man enough to handle her? She's grown up into one hell of a fine woman, Douglass. Only thing in my life I can honestly say I'm proud of."

There was a movement in the doorway and Brett glanced up, his heart turning over when his eyes met Kailin's. How long had she been standing there, he wondered? Had she heard that quiet admission of love from the old man she'd been battling for so long? Would she believe it if she had? "Have you told *her* that?"

"Hell, no. You can tell a woman she's beautiful, Douglass, because they expect that sort of thing. But never tell a woman she's smart—ruins 'em. You'll never get a word in edgeways from that day on."

Annoyance flitted through Kailin. Then she remembered the gentleness in her father's voice a few moments ago, the love in it, and had to laugh quietly. They were both like actors in some long-running play, mouthing the lines without even thinking about what they meant.

She shoved her hands into the pockets of her gray wool slacks and strolled into the firelight, oddly unsurprised at finding the two men she loved here, face-to-face. "You're a fraud, Daddy," she said with a hint of laughter in her voice. She put her hands on her father's shoulders and planted a kiss on his cheek. "And a disgusting chauvinist. You'd still have women's feet bound if you thought it would work."

"Biggest mistake we men ever made was giving women the vote," Yarbro growled. "How long have you been standing back there spying on me?"

"Long enough." She looked at Brett, smiling. "What brought you all the way up from Florida?"

"You know what brought me up here," he said softly.

Kailin's heart gave a slow somersault.

"He wants to marry you, Kailin," her father said.

"Do I have any choice in the matter, or have the two of you settled it between you over whiskey and a good cigar?"

"Your mother found my cigars and threw them out," Yarbro growled. He got to his feet, putting the robe and Maverick gently in the chair, and reached for the walking sticks. Kailin stepped toward him, but he gave her a ferocious glare and she subsided as he walked toward the door, slowly and with great determination. "For what it's worth, I think you should take him up on the offer," he said gruffly.

"I think I will," Kailin replied with a quiet laugh. "Thank you, Dad."

He looked at her for a long moment, the faintest hint of a smile playing around his mouth. The first breach in the barriers between them had been made; now it would simply be a matter of time.

His sharp gaze flicked away from hers to look at Brett. "I'll have a spare bed made up for you, Douglass. You may as well spend Thanksgiving with us, seeing as you're going to be marrying my daughter. A man should have his family around him on Thanksgiving.''

Kailin watched her father leave. When the door had closed, she sank into the chair and cradled Maverick in her lap, looking up at Brett. ''I think he's mellowing.''

''Like cider vinegar,'' Brett muttered, walking around the desk. He perched on one corner of it and looked down at her. ''Were you serious about marrying me?''

''Were you serious about asking me?''

''I've never been more serious about anything in my life. I let you get away from me eleven years ago, but I'm damned if it's going to happen again.'' He leaned over and cupped her chin in his hand, lifting her face so he could look into her eyes. ''I love you, Kailin McGuire.''

''I know,'' Kailin whispered. ''I've known for eleven years. But we just never seemed to be able to tell each other.''

''Well, I'm telling you now. I love you. I'll even put it in writing.'' He slipped a piece of elegant notepaper out of a holder on Yarbro's desk, then in a large but legible scrawl wrote, *I love you, Kailin McGuire*. He signed it with a flourish and handed it to her.

''I love you.'' She laughed, reaching up to pull him nearer. His mouth was honey-sweet and infinitely inviting, and she kissed him slowly and well.

''Here.'' He slipped a sheaf of papers out of his shirt pocket and put them in her hand.

Kailin looked at them curiously. ''What's this?''

''Paradise Point. The Land Use Committee approved Phase Three last night.'' He smiled. ''Thank you.''

''Why are you thanking me? Charlie Bryant was the one who bullied his board members into making all those concessions. It nearly killed them, but in the end they agreed it was better to go with smaller than not go at all. He was brilliant.''

"You were brilliant." He slipped off the desk and lifted her out of the chair before she could protest, then sat down and settled her comfortably in his lap.

Kailin ran her finger along his jawline, staring at him pensively. "I thought I'd lost you for good, Brett. It was almost as though you were fighting me, not letting me get close."

"I was." He smiled down at her. "Admitting I still loved you meant admitting that I'd made a terrible mistake eleven years ago. It was easier to think I'd been victimized, but the truth was that I was too scared to take a risk at loving you."

"Scared?" Kailin asked with a laugh. "You?"

"I was sure about everything in my life, Kailin—everything but you. That's why I believed what your father told me. I was so damned insecure—"

"Insecure?" Kailin looked at him in disbelief. "You were the most secure person I'd ever known!"

"About most things, maybe. But you intimidated the hell out of me. You were so beautiful and rich and . . . I don't know. Special, I guess. Unattainable. I couldn't figure out why you hung around with me. I didn't have a nice car, I couldn't take you to parties or fancy restaurants—hell, half the time I didn't have two cents to rub together. I kept telling myself that guys like me don't wind up with the fairy princess. Not in real life. I kept waiting for the clock to strike midnight, knowing I was crazy to fall in love with you. That sooner or later the fantasy would end."

"And then when it did . . ." Kailin touched his cheek.

"Marry me?" Brett whispered.

"With pleasure," Kailin whispered back.

"Good!" snapped a voice behind them. "Now that's settled, go start building me a dynasty. I'm not going to live forever, you know." Yarbro moved into view, eyes glinting. "And get out of my chair. Can't you see I'm crippled?"

Laughing, Brett got to his feet, Kailin still tight in his arms. "You heard the man," he murmured. "Would you like to build a dynasty with me?"

"I'd like nothing more." Kailin slipped her arms around his neck and nestled against him. "In fact," she murmured against his ear, "we could start right now if you've nothing more pressing to do. Mother's out for a while, and it's time for Daddy's medication and nap. No one will bother us for hours and hours."

"I love you."

"I know." She kissed his ear. "I have it in writing, remember?"

*   *   *   *   *

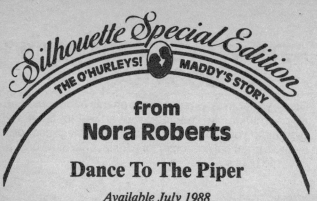

Silhouette Special Edition

THE O'HURLEYS! MADDY'S STORY

from
Nora Roberts

Dance To The Piper

Available July 1988

The second in an exciting new series about the lives and loves of triplet sisters—

If *The Last Honest Woman* (SE #451) captured your heart in May, you're sure to want to read about Maddy and Chantel, Abby's two sisters.

In *Dance to the Piper* (SE #463), it takes some very fancy footwork to get reserved recording mogul Reed Valentine dancing to effervescent Maddy's tune....

Then, in *Skin Deep* (SE #475), find out what kind of heat it takes to melt the glamorous Chantel's icy heart. Available in September.

THE O'HURLEYS!

**Join the excitement of
Silhouette Special Editions.**

SSE 463-1

ATTRACTIVE, SPACE SAVING BOOK RACK

Display your most prized novels on this handsome and sturdy book rack. The hand-rubbed walnut finish will blend into your library decor with quiet elegance, providing a practical organizer for your favorite hard-or soft-covered books.

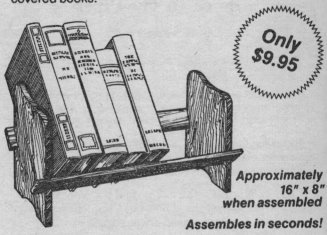

Only $9.95

Approximately 16" x 8" when assembled

Assembles in seconds!

To order, rush your name, address and zip code, along with a check or money order for $10.70* ($9.95 plus 75¢ postage and handling) payable to *Silhouette Books*.

Silhouette Books
Book Rack Offer
901 Fuhrmann Blvd.
P.O. Box 1396
Buffalo, NY 14269-1396

Offer not available in Canada.

*New York and Iowa residents add appropriate sales tax.

BKR-2A

 # Silhouette Desire

COMING NEXT MONTH

#439 THE CASTLE KEEP—Jennifer Greene
Although architect Micheal Fitzgerald had made a career out of building walls, he'd never seen defenses like Carra O'Neill's—defenses he planned on breaking down with a little Irish magic.

#440 OUT OF THE COLD—Robin Elliott
When Joshua Quinn was sent to protect Kristin Duquesne, he wasn't supposed to fall in love with her. But he had ... and now both their lives were in danger.

#441 RELUCTANT PARTNERS—Judith McWilliams
Elspeth Fielding had her own reasons for agreeing to live in a rustic cabin with James Murdoch. But after she met the reclusive novelist, the only important reason was him!

#442 HEAVEN SENT—Erica Spindler
A fulfilling career was Jessica Mann's idea of "having it all"—until she met Clay Jones and fulfillment took on a very different meaning.

#443 A FRIEND IN NEED—Cathie Linz
When Kyle O'Reilly—her unrequited college crush—returned unexpectedly, Victoria Winters panicked. She *refused* to succumb to her continuing attraction, but she could hardly kick him out—it was his apartment.

#444 REACH FOR THE MOON—Joyce Thies
The second of three *Tales of the Rising Moon*. Samantha Charles didn't accept charity, especially from the high and mighty Steven Armstrong, but a twist of fate had her accepting far more!

AVAILABLE NOW:

At Dodd Memorial Hospital, Love is the Best Medicine

When temperatures are rising and pulses are racing, Dodd Memorial Hospital is the place to be. Every doctor, nurse and patient is a heart specialist, and their favorite prescription is a little romance. This month, finish Lucy Hamilton's Dodd Memorial Hospital Trilogy with HEARTBEATS, IM #245.

Nurse Vanessa Rice thought police sergeant Clay Williams was the most annoying man she knew. Then he showed up at Dodd Memorial with a gunshot wound, and the least she could do was be friends with him—if he'd let her. But Clay was interested in something more, and Vanessa didn't want that kind of commitment. She had a career that was important to her, and there was no room in her life for any man. But Clay was determined to show her that they could have a future together—and that there are times when the patient knows best.